Selected for Bris...   ...risbane in
2004, this book he...

One Book One B...   ...d discuss
selected books. It ai...   ...ding in Brisbane
and create the atmos...   ...de book club.

One Book One Brisbane has become one of the most popular community events on Brisbane City Council's annual calendar. Activities include author talks and workshops, book discussions, book readings and storytimes at libraries.

For more information about **One Book One Brisbane**, visit www.ourbrisbane.com, your local library or phone Council on 3403 8888.

The **One Book One Brisbane** reading campaign helps to nurture an inclusive Brisbane, where everyone can take part in a city-wide book club and help achieve Council's vision for *Living in Brisbane 2010*.

Rebecca Sparrow was born in 1972 and lives in Brisbane. Every year she secretly stays up to watch the Eurovision Song Contest. *The Girl Most Likely* is her first novel.

You can visit Rebecca's website at
www.rebeccasparrow.com

the Girl Most Likely

A novel

REBECCA SPARROW

UQP

First published 2003 by University of Queensland Press
Box 6042, St Lucia, Queensland 4067 Australia
Reprinted 2003 (three times), 2004 (twice)

www.uqp.uq.edu.au

© Rebecca Sparrow

This book is copyright. Except for private study, research,
criticism or review, as permitted under the Copyright Act,
no part of this book may be reproduced, stored in a retrieval system,
or transmitted in any form or by any means without prior
written permission. Enquiries should be made to the publisher.

Typeset by University of Queensland Press
Printed in Australia by McPherson's Printing Group

Distributed in the USA and Canada by
International Specialized Book Services, Inc.,
5824 N.E. Hassalo Street, Portland, Oregon 97213–3640

Sponsored by the Queensland Office
of Arts and Cultural Development.

Cataloguing in Publication Data
National Library of Australia

Sparrow, Rebecca, 1972– .
　The girl most likely.

　　1. Young women — Fiction. 2. Separated women — Fiction. 3.
　Self-perception — Fiction. I. Title.

A823.4

ISBN 0 7022 3497 4

To Fred, Wendy and Rob Sparrow for love, encouragement, faith, endless cups of tea and the occasional lunch at the Oxo Towers.

"The only way is up. Baby."
Yazz and the Plastic Population

1

'Who's Anne Sneddon?'

It was a stupid question. One of those questions where the answer hits you as soon as the question mark has stepped off your lips. One of those times when you wished you could suck each single syllable back into your mouth and eat the moment, like Hannibal Lecter and his fava beans.

But you can't. I've asked. It's out there. And I'm going to pay for it. Miss Goulburn 1964, a.k.a Patricia Botham, would make sure of that.

Rachel!

She turns, eyebrows raised, and gives me "the look".

Things haven't gone well on this car trip. I close my eyes for a second and imagine that I'm somewhere more peaceful. But the sound of staccato horns and squealing tyres brings me sharply back to reality and the inside of the car I'm sitting in. My head slams backwards as our vehicle stops and catches its breath at the pedestrian crossing near the Valley Pool. A grandmother walks past. She glares at us. I don't blame her. Though it's upsetting that even nanna here has nailed a more intimidating "don't fuck with me" glare than me.

This car journey is making me feel nauseated. The driver is the problem. I contemplate opening the car door and tumbling MacGyver-style to freedom. Getting up close and personal with bitumen as the car races towards the airport is, at this point, more appealing than dealing with Patricia or this car journey.

Pity I'm driving.

But it's time to appease Patricia and deal with the Anne Sneddon issue.

'Anne Sneddon. Miss Australia 1979. I remember.'

And so we return to Patricia's favourite discussion. The discussion about beauty pageants. More specifically, why I, Rachel Hill, Patricia's twenty-seven-year-old daughter, primary school tunnel ball champion, St Peters prefect, Honours degree graduate, former magazine Features Editor, seemingly ideal candidate, have failed to succumb to the allure of the velvet cloak and the cubic zirconia crown.

Don't get me wrong, there was a period when I dreamt of the glamour and fame that only a dazzling smile, Farrah Fawcett hair, and a great pair of legs could bring, but I was seven at the time and my hair was more Velma than Daphne — from a *Scooby Doo* point of view. After the Channel Seven

Miss Australia telecast, I remember writing the newly crowned Anne Sneddon a letter telling her she was beautiful and asking her if she was a princess. Twenty-two days later I received a black and white signed official photo and a handwritten letter telling me that she hoped "all my dreams came true". Patricia was thrilled. I was thrilled. My classmates in 2H at Indooroopilly State School were thrilled. I spent the next eight days wearing a swimsuit, a Hungry Jacks crown and Mum's high heels to the dinner table.

But pretty soon I ditched the sequins fantasy for the clandestine appeal of an annex. I had decided that I wanted to be like Anne Frank (well, Anne Frank with a Hungry Jacks crown … it was hard to give up the glamour) and spent the ensuing weeks hiding in our loft, speaking in a dodgy accent that had more in common with *Hogan's Heroes* than a twelve-year-old Dutch girl. Unless Anne Frank's imaginary friend Kitty did say, 'I know nuthink' like Schultz. But I doubt it.

So while I flirted briefly with the notion of life on the pageant circuit in 1979, I haven't looked back since. Patricia, on the other hand, is still finding it hard to move on. She has always harboured dreams of me following in her footsteps and "taking up the challenge". And she loves Anne Sneddon. Her favourite Miss Australia. Partly because Anne was indeed as friendly as she was stunningly beautiful. Partly because she was the daughter of my father's secretary, Nan. But mostly because Patricia was crowned Miss Goulburn in 1964 and she feels like she, Anne and Shelley Porter from the newsagent at Kenmore Village (Murgon's Queen of Beef

1996) are all part of that special society. Title winners. Pageant Queens. Holders of the sceptre.

Me? I decline joining any club that today offers membership to pouty five-year-old girls with big Texan hair.

You're perfect. You'd win. Patricia smiles at me eagerly.

I wince. The Miss Brisbane Awards are currently recruiting in our area and she wants me to enter. If only she knew that this just wasn't possible.

'Forget it. So what days do I have to water the orchids?'

This is my cunning ploy to change topic. If Patricia is persistent about pageants, she is obsessive about her garden. And at times like this — when she's going away, I'm house-sitting and there's a need for her to give me instructions — she revels in handing out orders.

I've left you a note …

There's always a note.

… and why don't you clean out your old bedroom. Throw out what you can and move the rest up to the loft.

'No worries.'

Are you babysitting this week?

'Yep'.

Hmmm.

Patricia is not so keen on the idea of her eldest daughter, former Features Editor of Australia's largest travel magazine, working as a nanny to make ends meet.

Well, it won't hurt you to ring the agency and see if you could pick up some copy writing work a few days a week. You don't want to be sitting around the house all day, Rachel. You'll get bored.

'So the TV's broken?'

I've left the employment pages on the dining room table for you, just in case you want to have a look through them.

She looks at me with the face of a mother who wants her daughter to find a job. I look back at her with the face of a daughter who thinks matricide is dealt with a little too harshly by the current legal system.

We pull up to the "five minute drop off" zone of Brisbane International Airport. This is the cue for my father to awake from his drive-time nap – which, I know and he knows, he has been faking for the last 30 minutes. He knew better than to open his eyes, thus propelling him into the arena of pageant/employment/Anne Sneddon discussions.

I'll bring you back a Yorkie Bar, he says, giving me a sly wink as he unloads their bags onto a nearby trolley. *And I expect to have a best-seller to read when I get back.*

I smile and roll my eyes. I'd forgotten about the book. The book that I said I was going to write now that I'd quit my job. Good one Rachel.

'Give Caitlin a hug for me,' I say. 'And tell her I want my Laura Ashley jacket back and my Lenny Kravitz and Women in Docs CDs. Tell her that I know she took them. She's such a little…'

I want to swear.

'… pain.'

If I was with anyone other than my parents I would use the word *shit*. Caitlin is such a little *shit*. But if there's one rule I have with my parents, it's that I don't swear in front of them. Ever.

Never ever.

Okay, maybe once.

I swore in front of my mum when I was seventeen and I'd fallen asleep with my radio on. She came in and tried to turn off my radio by twiddling with the volume control. Being woken from my sleep by the thumping sounds of 'Onion Skin' by Boom Crash Opera, is what prompted the groan of 'Oh fucking hell Mum' as I reached down and switched off the radio myself, rolled over and went back to sleep.

The incident has never been spoken about.

Patricia has never attempted to turn off my radio again.

'… and have a wonderful time.'

We'll ring you when we get there, sweetheart. Look after yourself.

A few farewell hugs, some reminders about the Lean Cuisines in the freezer and they're disappearing through the door and over to the BA queue – ready to board Flight 16 that will take them to my little sister Caitlin in London. I sit back in the car and watch them for a while. I can tell Mum is nervous. She's checking and rechecking that her passport and tickets are safely in her handbag. My father is glancing over at the Exchange Bureau trying to decipher the current value of the Aussie dollar against the British pound. And then they're out of sight and my five minutes are up.

I turn back and stare at the dashboard and find myself singing along to Travis on the radio. And that's when I realise that I'm alone. My parents have gone. And despite the promise I made to the mirror this morning, I still didn't tell them I got married.

2

What would Mary do? It's a question that I ponder on the seventy-minute drive home. It's Friday evening, peak hour, as I crawl my way back through the city and eventually into the driveway of my childhood home in Kenmore.

What would Mary do?

Keys in hand, I walk through the front door, switch on the lights and realise the answer is obvious. Mary wouldn't do anything. Mary would never have gotten herself into this ridiculous situation in the first place. Nope. Mary and Rhoda definitely wouldn't have done it. Blair and Tootie and Jo wouldn't have done it. Laverne and Shirley wouldn't have done it … well Laverne might have but Shirley and

Carmine would have stopped her. So that just leaves me. Just me who would get married and not tell anyone.

As I brush past the hallway mirror I do my best perky smile to see if I, too, *sans* beret, could turn the world on with my smile. The bulb above me flickers and then goes dead.

It's hard to take a nothing day and suddenly make it all seem worthwhile when you're surrounded by pitch black.

I leave changing the bulb for later and move into the kitchen where the red light of hope is flashing. The 'you have friends' light of the answering machine. I've only been gone for two hours and there are two messages. The first message is a male voice I don't recognise.

This is a message for Rachel Hill. Rachel, it's Fergus McLaughlin from the Miss Brisbane Awards. We received your nomination yesterday. We don't usually take on entrants this late but your mother explained that you have special circumstances. Plenty more fish in the sea, love. So we'll be posting you out your introduction kit this afternoon. You should get it on Tuesday. There's details in there about our get together next Saturday at eleven am in our city office. So once you get the kit, give me a call back — my card is in there — just so I can confirm you'll be attending. Okay, thanks Rachel. Bye.

I can't believe she did this.

The second message starts playing. It's Satan.

Rachel, it's Mum. We're still waiting to board but I just thought that I should warn you that you might be getting a call from a young man called Fergus about the Miss Brisbane Awards. I registered you last week. You might be a few weeks behind the other girls but I just thought it would be good for you. A good way to meet some new friends and get out of the house. I don't want you sitting around moping over Troy.

I can hear Dad in the background asking Mum if she packed his eye drops.

Okay, I'd better go. Love you.

Troy.

My parents think that Troy and I have just broken up. Not gotten married. Not about to get divorced. Just broken up. That's a strange expression, a stupid way to describe it. 'Just broken up' reduces a three-year relationship to sounding like a piece of crockery that's been smashed on the kitchen floor after you've done the washing up. As if you were even one piece to begin with. Or maybe that's what it's like for other people. Just not us.

I fix myself a scotch and dry and get the envelope, with its California postmark, out of my handbag. I read over the papers again. The sections that need my signature have been highlighted with a fluoro yellow pen.

Troy.

I pick up a pen and let it hover over the fluoro markings like a mozzie that's trying to decide between landing on ankle or thigh. But I can't seem to make myself do it. Maybe later. But not now. Not right this minute. I'll change my marital status tomorrow. And I take the envelope and put it in a place where I know I'll find it again easily.

Eventually I pick up my drink and walk into my childhood bedroom. A room that is still celebrating 1987. I hear the bedroom walls wheeze, laden with memorabilia from my life. Memories stuffed into Clarks shoe boxes and Ekka showbags. Memories that have been folded up and crammed into desk drawers or been punctured by old tacks and left hanging from corkboards. Memories perched atop my wooden CopperArt hat stand, stained by the smell of Australis and 4711 perfume; some slightly faded but still crystal clear, others loose and limp like a piece of hat elastic that has lost its will to live.

Looking around, I feel like I have stepped into the life of an old friend. An old friend with a slightly unhealthy obsession with A-Ha.

It's not that I haven't been home in a while. Up until last week, when I was living in my flat, I was over here once a week for a meal. But that's not the same. I haven't lived here. In this house. In this bedroom. I've breezed in and out, when I've been looking for passports or old photos but, like a fair-weather friend, I've never stopped and chewed the fat with my former self. Maybe it's because we have so little in common these days.

I lie down on my single bed and hold my old pillow to my face, inhaling the smells of my childhood. I feel comforted. And I end up lying there for an hour. Thinking about Troy. Thinking about Troy and contemplating the paradox of living life as a divorcee in a bedroom full of Morten Harket posters.

When I pictured twenty-seven, it didn't look like this. I was "the girl most likely to succeed". This is not what was meant to happen.

For the next two days I exist in something of a haze. I dig up my Fido Dido pyjamas, camp out in the living room and watch TV for two days straight, only getting up and leaving the room to **a)** use the bathroom or **b)** discover new foods that taste better with Miracle Whip. That's a no for Maggi Two Minute Noodles, toast and Thai Chicken Lean Cuisine and a yes for broccoli, oven chips and plain, lightly salted Thins.

In those two days I buy the entire series of Tai-Bo tapes and something called the Hairdini Magic Styling Wand. I dig out Patricia's Bedazzler and shoot rhinestones all over five tea-towels, an apron, an old t-shirt and some tracksuit pants. I become addicted to Open Learning, stay up every night to watch Letterman and finally work out what Kenneth Copeland's *Hour of Power* is all about. I sleep a lot and eat a lot. And I feel like crap. But I'm married crap so that at least raises me one notch above the type of poo that can't find a husband.

I let every phone call go through to Patricia's "we're on holidays" answering machine message. Fergus McLaughlin has left another message asking me to confirm my Miss Brisbane nomination and I've ignored it. Mum and Dad have rung to let me know that they've arrived safely and that Caitlin has her nose pierced. Zoë has rung three times begging me to read her latest literary masterpiece. Her third and final message consisted of Zoë just moaning *Piiiiiiiiiii-iiiiiiiiiiick Uuuuuuuuuuuup* over and over until the tape ran out.

Zoë Budd is my best friend. We've known each other since we were five. Mrs Roberts sat us next to each other on our first day of Grade One and before the day was out we were singing Leif Garrett songs and discussing the greatness of *H.R. Pufnstuf*. Twenty-two years later and she's still skinny as a rake, still sports a tangle of brunette ringlets and still has a smile so wide she may as well have a coat hanger in her mouth. She has the face of Elisabeth Shue and the manners of Veruca Salt. But best of all she's the proud owner of Brisbane's filthiest laugh. She laughs like someone who's just committed a crime and gotten away with it. I love her like a sister. She'll tell me when I've got food in my teeth. Shout me a beer when I'm skint. And even though she always beats me at Trivial Pursuit, she pretends that I let her win.

I love her like a sister but she's definitely not a writer. Zoë is a Flight Centre travel agent. A travel agent who, in her spare time, enters erotic fiction competitions. Which is fine. The only problem is that Zoë has never won. Never won, never got a place, never even been highly commended. This is because what Zoë thinks is erotic fiction would actually be classed as porn. Very bad, dirty porn. Far from being a turn-on, Zoë's writing is the type of porn that would turn the stomachs of the judges who read Zoë's entries. The type of porn that makes you clench your bottom and cross your legs. Porn that could turn you off sex for the rest of your life.

But I don't have the heart to tell her. So I just proofread her pieces and tell her when she's spelt faeces wrong and when she's used more goldfish/olive oil scenarios than usual. For a garden-variety lesbian, Zoë's got some serious issues with goldfish.

By five p.m. on Sunday, I decide it's time to make contact with the outside world again. Plus, there's nothing on TV. I ring Zoë. She tells me to get ready and that she'll pick me up in ten minutes. She wants to go to the RE, the Royal Exchange Hotel. Fifteen minutes later there's a knock on the door.

'Hey.'

What the hell happened to you?

I stare at her blankly. I have answered the door in my Fido Dido ensemble, complete with sheepskin slippers. And there's a distinct possibility that the corners of my mouth are caked in baked bean stains.

And what the hell are you wearing? You look like shit.

I blink at her.

You've been in your pyjamas all day, haven't you? She pushes past me and walks into the house to survey the crime scene.

Jesus, Hill. She strides through to the kitchen, where she begins picking up indiscriminate items and naming them out loud, as if she's part of a TV show forensic team. Half-emptied, defrosted packet of fish fingers lying in the sink, check. Half-eaten can of baked beans, check. Stale corn chips, check. Lean Cuisine packets and Tupperware container of slightly dodgy-smelling spaghetti sauce, check. Open tin of Milo with teaspoon sitting inside it, check.

There's a chalk outline of my former self on the floor.

Book 'em Danno.

She turns off the television.

So did you tell them?

'Put it this way. Patricia's entered me in the Miss Brisbane Awards. So that'd be a *no*.'

Cool. You'd win. You're the original over-achiever.

'Hello? It's MISS Brisbane. I think I'd be disqualified on a minor technicality.'

Yeah. Right. She picks up an old photo of me, Caitlin, Mum and Dad taken on a trip to London in the late seventies. I'm four and wearing some funky hipsters and a striped, big-collared shirt. Caitlin is two and is wearing a floral flannelette dress, the bottom of which she's clutching with one small hand and pulling up to her waist, revealing her knickers while she sucks her thumb. She still does that. Lifting up her dress and flashing her knickers, not sucking her thumb.

Zoë puts the frame back on the shelf, next to the tribe of other family snapshots.

You're going to have to tell them.

'I know.'

Zoë looks at me intently. I try to regain some dignity by scraping the baked beans off the corner of my mouth with my tongue.

You know you're going to be okay. You've just got to get focused and start …

I give Zoë my 'I'm not in the mood for a lecture' face but she soldiers on regardless.

It's been a month since you quit the magazine — you've got to start writing again. You can't just hide out here. I mean, I know I told you that you should just chill out for a while and kick back but you've got to DO something. Eventually.

I poke my tongue out at her.

Fine. Go get ready. Jeans, grey t-shirt, boots — go!

I march upstairs and get dressed. I can hear Zoë cleaning up the kitchen, putting things back in their rightful spots and chucking other stuff in the bin.

I'm glad that Zoë knows. About the marriage. It makes it easier. Even when we don't talk about it, her knowing just helps me deal with it. And I haven't been dealing with it so well lately. Troy told a heap of people on his side of the world. Family and friends, because he was so excited. But I didn't really want to share it. So Zoë is the only person I told. Well, Zoë and a lady called Ruby who sat next to me on the flight home from Vegas. So it's just the two of them. A perfect stranger and a girl I've known my entire life and what's funny is that their reaction was the same. *You were drunk, right?* That was the first question. *It was a spur of the moment decision, wasn't it?* That's the other one. And when you answer 'no' to both of those, the look on their face, in their eyes, said it all. That's the thing about Vegas weddings. They seem really funny on sitcoms and in the movies but in real-life it's a little different. Harder to explain. Not quite so many punchlines as an episode of *Friends*.

I go back to looking in the mirror. It occurs to me that the good thing about unwashed hair is that it goes into a ponytail more easily. I pride myself on finding the positive. I pull on my trademark baseball cap, slap on some makeup and survey the results.

I look like Kate Winslet on crack. No. I look like someone

who's about to get divorced. I look like someone who's about to get divorced, who's lost control of their life.

I notice a twenty-cent piece on the floor of my bedroom. *Heads* my life will work out. *Tails* it's going to be shit. I toss the coin a little too hard. It retaliates by running for cover under my bookshelf as soon as it hits the floor. Bugger. I go downstairs, grab my keys and leave. And as we're heading out the door Zoë asks me why there is a big yellow envelope sitting under the jar of Miracle Whip in my fridge.

My head hurts. And the alarm clock is ringing. The worst possible combination for a Monday morning. An "Alex" morning. A morning when I am supposed to reincarnate as a perky, chirpy Mary Poppins. Instead I look withered and smell like the Castlemaine Fourex Brewery tour.

I jump out of bed and head for the shower. I should never have gone out with Zoë last night. Sunday nights at the RE are always a little insane. And Zoë decided it was a lick, sip, suck tequila kinda night.

I grab a handful of Froot Loops, lock the front door, and point my 1990 Mazda in the direction of Brookfield. It's 6.53am. I have seven minutes to get there on time. I'm about to pull out of the driveway when I notice a young woman pushing a stroller along. Inside is a baby dressed like a bumblebee: little yellow-and-black-striped hat with matching jacket. A baby with plump, rosy cheeks and a kiss for a mouth. A baby that looks like it's on its way to an Anne Geddes audition. The woman pushing the stroller couldn't be any older than me. And she's a mother.

For a moment I stop the car and just sit. I wonder if that's the problem. That I've never had *that*. That whole baby cluckiness thing. I mean, I've done my fair share of high-school babysitting but I just never felt it. That burning need to have one of my own. One that was mine, that had my eyes or my mouth, that I could dress up like a doll and wheel around in a pram all day, talking to it about the weather, and how cute it looks in its little beanie hat and what we're going to have for tea. And I wonder if Troy could sense it. If deep down he didn't think I had it in me. That Rachel Hill isn't the maternal, mothering type. And who's to say that Troy would be wrong?

The truth is that when other girls, like Caitlin, were playing with Baby Alive or Barbie, I was writing plays or playing Frogger on the Atari or trying to catch bees with an old tea-towel or building cheese mazes for local skinks or setting ants on fire using a magnifying glass and a blazing sun. I was doing a million things, none of which involved nappies or formula or little pink plastic shoes. And the more time I've spent with my friends who have children, the more I thought they were a pain. Well, not a pain, wrong word. Babies just seemed like a hassle. All the crying for a start. All those tears. And those scrunched up little red faces and those little hands forming little fists. And all that poo. I remember last year when Jane roped me into looking after her baby, Georgina. She was a pooing machine. But then, in fairness to Georgina, if you're shovelling pureed pumpkin and spinach into the top, it's little wonder that it's going to reappear out the bottom. The exit-only end. The "right back at ya, serves you right for feeding me that crap" end. Sure. Georgina was trying to tell me something. Like maybe, "Next time try giving me pizza."

I've never really been big on kids. Until I met Alexandria. But then, Alex is completely different. She's six. She can burp hello. And she can read newspaper headlines backwards. And, if I knot the rope to make it shorter, she can skip really, really fast when she's concentrating hard and when Emma (her best friend) isn't throwing Tiny Teddy biscuits at her head.

Alex came into my life sort of by accident. I needed a job. Alex needed someone to take her to school and make her a lunch that didn't include sandwiches or fruit or boxes of sultanas disguised as a fun kids snack. She needed someone who would be available to come and look at her paintings when they get pinned up on the walls of her Grade Two classroom, someone to help her carry her Lego masterpieces to her class when it's her turn for show and tell. Someone to help her put on her ballet stockings, and tie up her shoelaces and brush her hair and remind her that the word "like" is different to the word "lick", when she's reading her latest Digger book. And since Sharon, her mum, is at work all of the time and since Sharon can't be there to do any of these things, the agency recommended me and I got the job.

So that's how it happened. One minute I was registering for baby-sitting work with Dial-An-Angel. The next minute I was agreeing to look after Alex every morning before school and on the occasional afternoon when Sharon can't get away from the studio in time for the three o'clock bell.

I started last Monday.

It was the longest week of my life.

Alex and I didn't exactly hit it off straight away. I'm hoping it's a little better now. I walked into the lounge on that first morning and she was curled up in a chair, in her favourite pink nightie, watching TV with Snowy her cat on her lap. 'Hello there!' I said in my chirpiest, kid-friendly voice. She didn't even flinch. Didn't even cast me a sideways glance. Kids are like dogs: they smell your fear. She wasn't about to make this easy. 'Hello there, Alex, what are you and Snowy watching?' I said again. Again trying my best not to give her any hint that I was nervous.

Too late.

She just glared up at me from beneath her scrappy brown fringe and said, *We're watching* Blue's Clues. And she said it in a surly, cutting tone. A tone that belonged to Bernard King, not a kid in Grade Two. And then she turned back to the TV and that cartoon puppy. A puppy who, frankly, wouldn't know a clue if it bit him on the arse.

A week later and Alex tolerates my presence and treats me with suspicion and I do my best to remember that she likes the chocolate not apple & cinnamon Poptarts.

But no matter how cranky she is towards me, I can't help but like her. She says what she thinks. She's not ashamed to ask for a peanut butter and honey sandwich with the crusts cut off. She openly defends reality TV shows. She walks around the house saying that she still can't believe that people voted for GST. But what I like about Alex the most is that no matter how much she pretends to hate me, she still instinctively reaches up and holds my hand when we cross the road. And her eyes light up when I tell her that I think she's smart.

So while last week wasn't so good for us, this week is going to be different. This week we're going to get along. I'm going to win her over. I can feel it.

Please God let us get along.

By the time nine am rolls around I have worked out that either

(a) God's not that keen on me, or

(b) God is partially deaf like Zoë's Gran.

Because despite my desperate prayer, this morning was not a good morning. The high point was Alex refusing to go to school unless she could keep the fake tattoo on her forehead that she'd stuck there on the weekend. The low point was Alex bursting into tears when I told her off for feeding her poached egg to Snowy under the table.

I get home at ten am and I'm exhausted. I plonk my keys on the kitchen table and decide that it's time to survey Patricia's note.

Water the plants, put the bin out, clean out my bedroom. Clean out my bedroom? Too boring. I keep reading down the list. Remember that there's Lean Cuisines in the freezer, ring the agency, and then there's something about Margaret from next door. Mum's written 'Be nice to Margaret when you see her. She's just split up from her husband and she's taking it badly.'

I don't even know who Margaret is. I think she lives in the house behind us. I do recall Patricia saying once that someone called Margaret spends a lot of time crying these days. That must be her. If I see someone who looks a little down I make a pledge to smile and act neighbourly.

Which makes me feel like Samantha Stevens from *Bewitched*. But I seriously doubt that Samantha Stevens would have married someone to save an ailing long-distance relationship. Nope. That would just be me again. Just me.

I decide that I will clean out my old bedroom. And I think seriously about doing that as I grab the box of Froot Loops and plop down on the couch to watch *Good Morning Australia*.

4

I have discovered that if you eat too many Froot Loops they hurt your mouth. Just like Coco-Pops. At five pm on Monday evening I decide to write to Kellogg's and make them aware of this dilemma.

I go to the computer and whip up the following complaint.

> **Dear Kellogg's**
> I have long been a fan of your work. However I feel that it is imperative to inform you that your product, Froot Loops, has the capacity to damage the roof of the consumer's mouth. It appears that said 'Loop' is actually quite sharp and when indulging in the cereal as a dry meal, the consumer can end up injured after a few successive hours of eating.

Should you wish to amend this matter, I will happily receive free product at the above listed address.
Sincerely
Rachel Hill (B.B.Comm)

I ring Zoë at work and tell her about my letter. She hangs up on me.

I have wasted another entire day watching TV, bedazzling tea-towels and writing letters of complaint about children's cereal.

I think about Patricia's list. I could go and clean out my bedroom or I could get something to eat.

I stand in front of the open fridge and survey the contents, scanning for new snack ideas. And then I notice the yellow envelope, which is now nicely chilled and has a ring mark where the Miracle Whip was sitting on it. The papers. I choose to ignore them and decide instead that it's time to clean out my room.

Four and a half hours later and I have three garbage bags of rubbish and two cartons of stuff to be stored up in our loft. It's 1.03am and my legs ache from sitting cross-legged on the floor for so long. The whole process wasn't as bad as I thought it would be. In fact, for the first couple of hours I was whizzing through my belongings with LA-Riots-style heartless glee.

Fluoro shoelaces, keep.

The Web of Life biology textbook, chuck.

A-Ha/21 Jump Street poster collection, keep.

Phil Collins, 'No Jacket Required' cassette, chuck but play it once first, lip-synching in the mirror to Billy Don't Lose My Number.

Slinky, keep.

Strawberry Shortcake Doll with no smell left, chuck.

'Xanadu' soundtrack, keep.

Grade 7 'The Foods of Alsace-Lorraine' French assignment, chuck.

Dolly magazines (1984–1989), chuck.

Weird Al Yankovic poster, keep.

Smurf collection, keep.

Polka dotted tea-towel used in catching bees unawares, keep.

Slightly faded Hungry Jacks crown circa 1979, keep.

Hungry Hungry Hippos game with damaged hippo head, chuck.

I even found my first diary. Hard cover with little blue and pink flowers, ruled pages with a love heart next to the space where you're meant to write the date and a piss-weak lock that any big brother could pick open. I brush off the dust. I remember when I got this. It was Christmas 1986, the same year that "Santa" gave me a Chess for Beginners book, a bike helmet and Debbie Gibson's Electric Youth album. Some years Santa really shits me.

That's when I saw it sticking out from under a pile of Archie comics. The shoebox. I recognised it instantly, even though it's been nearly a decade since I've seen it. Written in faint blue biro, in bubble writing, are the words 'awards and achievements'. A nice neat little title for a shoebox that a seventeen-year-old Grade Twelve student decided to file her accomplishments in. And at 1.03am, sitting cross-legged on my bedroom floor, I am holding this box, debating the wisdom of opening it. But the lid comes off despite my reservations.

The first thing that I see is my Prefect's badge. I pin it on and look at myself in the mirror. I wasn't one of those girls who was chosen to be a Prefect because they're really popular with the entire school. I wasn't chosen because I could run the 100m faster than anyone else or because I was in a Zone Netball Team — I couldn't and I wasn't. I was chosen because I was smart and well-behaved and responsible. I was chosen because the teachers knew I was an achiever, that I did the right thing, that I wasn't easily led astray. They chose me because I was the girl most likely to succeed — the girl who won most competitions she entered, who could have a laugh and a joke with her class mates and still get top marks in biology and French. The girl who was destined to be something. The Webster dictionary's definition of a success:

> success (suc ses) **n. 1.** *a)* a favourable result; an event that accomplishes its intended purpose *b)* something having a favourable outcome. **2.** the gaining of wealth, fame etc. **3.** a person with a record of successes who doesn't fuck up by getting married in Las Vegas by an Elvis impersonator. [syn: winner] [ant: loser, see R. Hill]

I glance over the remaining contents of the shoebox. Westpac Maths Competition certificates. Report cards that don't get much further than the first letter of the alphabet.

Duke of Edinburgh Awards Scheme achievements. The Barbara Kingsford Harris Award for Service to the School. Netball pendants. Choir certificates. Flinders House Tunnel Ball ribbons.

People say "your school days are the best days of your life". And I'm beginning to think that's true for the school captains and prefects. And I'm beginning to wonder what would happen if she met me today. If I ran into this girl, this seventeen-year-old girl who now resides in the shoebox, the girl most likely to succeed. Would she look at me with pity in her eyes? Or scorn? And would she wonder at what point along the line I got it so wrong? Wonder how I deviated from the plan. And I'd try to impress her with my work on the magazine and how I'd been promoted to Features Editor so quickly. And I'd show her the article I did on flamenco dancing in Buenos Aires that everyone said was brilliant and nearly got turned into a story on *Getaway*. And I'd try to explain how things happened the way they did. How easy it is to make a wrong decision, choose the wrong path. But I suspect that she would just look at me, in my grey tracksuit pants with my lank unwashed hair and walk away, hoping that she'd never run into me again. She'd walk away thinking "I'm a Prefect. I can't believe that's how I end up. What a loser".

I start to wonder how I got to this point. When the majority of my friends are in stable relationships, how did I end up alone and unhappy with a husband that nobody knows about who lives on the other side of the world? But I *had* it. I had the great job and the great guy and somewhere along the line I fucked up. My grip loosened. And now I'm stuck with this version of my life. And I don't want this. I don't want any part of this. I'm the one who's supposed to have the life that goes with the Ikea catalogue. I'm supposed to be spending my weekends choosing between the solid beech Kronvik Dining Table with matching woven chairs and the solid wood (with a patina finish) Visdalen glass door cabinet. When birthday dinners and weddings come around, I want to be getting invitations that have two names on them and don't say 'Rachel and Friend', or, worse still, just 'Rachel'. I want to go back to having someone to come home to at the end of the day who cares about whether or not I had lunch or had a headache in the morning that went away by eleven am. I want my own flat. And a career that I love, that I'm good at. And I want to be a success. Again. I want things to go back to the way they were when all my friends envied me and said things like, *Isn't Rachel amazing? How does she do it?* Because they used to say that. Once. It's just been a while since I heard it.

Part of me wants to blame Troy. I want to see him and scream at him, 'Why are you ruining everything? Because everything was going okay, everything was going according to plan and now you've fucked it up for me.' But no matter how much I want to hate Troy I don't think I'll ever be able to. Although his timing could have been better. The day I quit my job and announce to the world that I'm moving to the States is the day Troy decides to leave the message. The *don't resign* message. The *we need to talk because this isn't going to work out* message on my answering machine. Broken heart aside, I was too proud to ask for my job back. Which left me with my pride but no weekly salary to pay the rent. But that was a couple of months ago. I'm here now. I have to move on.

And that's when I see the goals. Folded up and tucked away at the bottom of the box. I take the folded piece of paper out. It's been typed and was written on my last day of Year 12 at St Peters.

Things to Achieve Before I Turn 28
1. Be able to speak French
2. Have travelled to Paris, Rome, New York and London
3. Have one article published in a magazine or newspaper
4. Be married to a man who makes me go weak at the knees
5. Be able to waltz properly
6. Be able to play 'Jessica's Theme' on the piano

I don't even remember writing these. God knows what prompted me to do it but it's been witnessed by Zoë as evident by her ridiculously flowery signature on the bottom of the page. Although, now that I look at her signature closely, I can see that she's signed it Zoë Perkins not Zoë Budd. Miss Perkins was our PE teacher.

I go through the list over and over. On a Monday night in October, a decade after this list was written, it suddenly seems vital that I work out how many of these things I have achieved. How much of it I can cross off. Within minutes I realise that theoretically I have achieved every goal bar the last two. I can't really waltz. And despite having had piano lessons for six years and having watched *The Man From*

Snowy River more than thirty-four times, I still don't know how to play 'Jessica's Theme'.

So I've done all the goals except two. And I achieved number four by default. Okay. Two still left. I think about this. I decide to give myself a conceded pass on the waltzing since I did take lessons a while ago, and while I may not be great, I can get through an entire song without breaking any toes. I feel a little guilty but I cross it off the list. So that just leaves the last goal. Playing 'Jessica's Theme'. This bothers me. I go to bed but I can't sleep. I feel agitated.

I go downstairs, put on some Jeff Buckley and start up the computer. I read a few emails that have been sent to me from friends overseas and then find myself plugging IQ Tests into my metacrawler search engine. Three pages of sites come up. I spend the next two hours and forty-five minutes deciphering numerical sequences, calculating percentages and analysing Venn diagrams. I take three separate tests from three different sites. My average score is 130.

What am I thinking? Do I actually think that if I get a good score that it makes everything all right? Am I so stupid, so pathetic that I would think that a score of 130 is some kind of sign, an indicator that I can get myself out of this mess? Or do I just think that a three-digit number lets me off the hook somehow. Proves that I'm not responsible for the fucked-up state my life is in. "Could have happened to anyone. See? I didn't mean to go into a Vegas chapel and get married. Can't you tell? I've got an IQ of 130."

I'm so fucking stupid.

I lie down on the floor of the study and cry myself to sleep. Jeff sings on.

5

Tuesday morning I feel hollow. Empty. I feel like the reality of the situation has finally hit me and no IQ test result, or Hairdini for that matter, is going to change anything.

At the Moore's house, even Alex notices that I'm a bit down. Her remedy is to perform an impromptu ballet concert in her nightie in the kitchen, while I pack her lunchbox. As her encore, she wants to show me how fast she can skip now. She's been practising. As the doorknob and I turn the rope, I tell her that I think she would skip even faster if she put Snowy down first. But she insists that Snowy loves skipping as much as she does. Snowy looks unconvinced. Or at least he would look unconvinced if his face and arms weren't squashed up against Alex's chest quite so hard. And, as if to prove a point at the end of the skip-a-thon, Snowy promptly walks sideways into the lounge room and vomits all over Sharon's knitting. Alex looks at the vomit. Then at Snowy. And then says *Bad Snowy* in her angry monster voice, waving her right hand in his face and then clipping him on the head.

And then she picks up the rope and skips off into the distance.

Snowy looks at me, as if to say 'skipping sucks'. And I'm left wondering how to get cat spew out of a mohair Broncos scarf.

When I get home there is another message from Fergus McLaughlin of the Miss Brisbane Awards. It appears that my refusal to return his calls has left Fergus McLaughlin suspect about my willingness to compete, so his message gets my attention. Apparently, if I want to get a refund on Patricia's initial registration fee of $150 then I have to turn up in person to Saturday's "entrant get together" to get it. I am cheered up briefly at the prospect of gaining $150 but my mind keeps harking back to last night's discovery.

I go up to my bedroom and try to read a book. I choose something that will provide some escapism. But I can't seem to get past the part where Charlotte has written "Some Pig" in the doorway of the barn.

Then I get an idea.

My ideas suck.

In my despair I'd remembered an episode of *Oprah* where she says the best way to feel better and get in touch with your authentic self is to go through old magazines and make a "you" collage. Cut out pictures of things that you like, things that speak to you, the guest collage-maker said. Oprah had nodded earnestly. Cut out pictures and captions and words that symbolise your goals and your dreams, they said. This seemed like a good idea. So I headed back to the newsagent and, using my impending $150 refund, bought $91 worth of magazines and a big piece of white cardboard for the 'clag and mag' version of me.

I spend an hour flipping through *Tatler, Who Magazine, Cleo, Cosmo, In Style, Marie Claire, New Woman, Hello, B, Red* and *Vogue*. In the process I learn how to dress five kilos lighter, how to make pumpkin risotto, how to tell if he's "The One" and "Why These Three Women Are In Love With Convicted Murderers". But the only thing that I cut out is a picture of Minnie Driver's breasts. What can I say, I'm a 12B.

That's when it dawns on me. I have no choice. I have to learn 'Jessica's Theme'. Yes. It's a good starting point for me. A good way to demonstrate that I am still in control, I'm still the same old me, I'm still achieving. And I'm not just going to learn it. I'm going to learn it perfectly. Off by heart. Because that will be a sign. If I can master this piece of music, if I can have the discipline and the drive to learn it, then things can't be as bad as they seem.

But I need a proper timeline. Oprah says a goal is no good unless it has an expiry date attached to it. So I write it in big letters on my piece of white cardboard in an artline pen.

I will play 'Jessica's Theme' perfectly, off by heart, by 30 October.

Which just happens to be my twenty-eighth birthday. That gives me exactly three weeks and I am going to achieve this goal if it kills me.

I find the music stored in the piano seat between my old Beginner's Book and my Can't Stop the Hits Volume Twelve Piano Book. It's nice to know that should I ever want to play 'Holiday', I have the music ready and waiting.

It's been a little while since I've sat down and played Mum and Dad's electric piano. Eight years. But surely playing the piano is like riding a bike. You never forget.

Two hours of piano practice later I realise that playing the piano when you haven't played for eight years is nothing like riding a bike. Nothing at all.

7

I play until my fingers ache. Until my eyes can barely focus on the already overly scrutinised sheets in front of me. I play until my mind goes blank. I play until my brain is full of off-key tunes and jumbled phrasing. I play while my stomach rumbles and my eyes long to close. I play until I get it *right*.

But I don't get it right.

This piece is taunting me. I fumble with the keys like a fifteen-year-old boy and his girlfriend's bra. My fingers refuse to do as they are told. The tune in my head barely matches what is coming from the lounge room. I wonder if it's too late to ditch this goal and find a tunnel ball team in search of a captain.

On Wednesday I keep practising. I practise for five hours

straight. Mastering 'Jessica's Theme' is all I can think about. For some reason I feel like everything is riding on this. I have no choice. I've got to get it right. I keep practising.

I'm getting irritable. The metronome has taken to tsk-tsking me instead of keeping my pace. I am getting nowhere and I have a smart-arse metronome to deal with.

I play the bars over and over and over. Every time I screw up, I start again. I keep screwing up. Making obvious errors. Missing chords. Hitting wrong keys. As if to tease me the tune plays perfectly in my head all through the day. I can hear it as I fold the washing, hear it when I am brushing my hair or cleaning my teeth. Hear it when I am flipping through the Miss Brisbane Awards info that has arrived in the mail. It plays over and over in my mind. I just can't seem to pin it down.

I try a change of tack and take out my Beginner's Book. A book bursting with nursery rhymes and warm-up exercises. A book whose sole purpose is to humiliate adult-learners. I flip through the pages and choose 'Happy Frog'. Perhaps I just need to relax, I say to myself. And so I spend an hour relaxing with 'Happy Frog' and not being able to play it all the way through without making an error. Not once. If I met this frog, I would wipe the damn smile off his face.

Then Zoë rings.

What are you doing?

'Letting a frog break my spirit.'

I forgot to tell you that Dave Howard is doing a book signing tomorrow night at Indooroopilly.

'Is he? What time?'

Six pm. We should go. It'll be great fun. We can get him to sign our copies of 'August Moon'.

'Remember when we saw him once at the Toowong Night Owl buying milk? Remember that? He looked really nice. Didn't he? He seems friendly. I bet he's friendly.'

Sure. Sure he's friendly. He's not that famous yet. He's still down-to-earth. I saw him interviewed once on Brisbane Extra. *He looks like he's friendly. He looks like he'd be a regular funny type of twenty-something guy. We should definitely do this. I could pick you up at 5.20 and then we can be there a little bit early ...*

'Right. Because even though he's not really well known there could be crowds.'

Yeah. Exactly. You never know. And we should definitely take our books and get them signed.

'Yeah.'

I gotta go. I'll see you tomorrow.

I fall asleep at one am. I dream that I am Jessica Harrison and I am riding through the Victorian bush with the wind blowing in my air. And then Jim Craig comes and finds me and he takes me in his arms and tells me that my piano playing sucks. I wake up, it's 5.47 am and I go back to practise before leaving the house for my date with Alex.

At ten o'clock, I'm back. I sit down at the keyboard. Ready to practise. Ready to play this piece perfectly. Ready to win the competition between me and this sheet of music. I methodically flatten down the music in front of me, as if I have spit in my hand and am smoothing down the hair of a small child. I spend nearly a minute pressing the pages down firmly, smoothing out any wrinkles or bends, running those kinks out of town, like a sheriff in a spaghetti western. Then I decide never to do that again because frankly it's a little creepy.

Okay. I do my warm-up exercises like a professional. Fingers stretched, shoulders back, sitting up straight. I'm ready. Music is my world. I pretend that I have an audience. I am the Vanessa Mae of the piano world. Vanessa Mae of the piano world whose repertoire consists solely of 'Happy Frog'. I place my fingers on the keys and prepare to concentrate on the amphibian and his mood.

And now, for my next piece, 'La Grenouille Heureux'.

And I launch into the most dizzying 'Happy Frog' rendition that has ever been played. There are highs, there are lows. I convey all of it. I nail the Frog. Yesterday the Frog had sounded melancholy, depressed even. But not today. Today that Frog is drunk on happy. The audience cheers in my mind and I pretend that I am considering an encore performance, but this time it will be 'Happy Frog' accompanied by a Bossa Nova rhythm.

Eventually, when the Frog has exhausted every single Latin beat available to him, I get out the piece. I am revved up from the Frog so I am feeling that this is possible — today is the day that I get through the first couple of bars of 'Jessica's Theme' *sans* error.

And that's when I hear it.

At first I'm a little confused and I assume that the music coming from outside somewhere is just the tune that's playing in my head. But it's not. I push my hair back behind my ears, as if a few strands of hair have the power to totally distort sounds. I sit there, at my keyboard, staring at the keys as I strain to listen. I don't believe it.

Someone is playing 'Jessica's Theme'.

Someone is playing 'Jessica's Theme'. And it's not me.

The reason I know this is because this other person isn't making a mistake in the first bar. I jump up from the piano stool and start pacing around the house, going in and out of rooms, trying to work out where the music is coming from. And all I can think is that someone's been listening to me practise and now they're making fun of me. One of the neighbours has been home during the day, they've been listening to me grind out this damn piece hour after hour. And now they're mocking me. I feel sick.

I walk in and out of rooms, as if there's a chance I might be able to see something, spot a clue in my house. I wish I could tell where it's coming from. But I can't pinpoint it. I stand out on the veranda. I think I can tell which direction the sound is coming from.

It stops.

So I wait. And wait. And wait. Nothing. I go back inside. My heart is racing. What the hell just happened here? I sit at the kitchen bench and start trying to recall the names of the neighbours. I am forced to admit that I have taken little notice in recent years of Patricia's ramblings about which neighbour is going halves in a new fence, which neighbour's dog keeps barking late at night and which neighbours mow their lawn far too early on a Sunday morning. I know that people have come and gone over the years. Places have been rented out. Families have grown up and moved on. The only real neighbour whose name I know is Margaret-the-cryer and I don't even know for sure which house she lives in. Fuck.

I go back and look at the piano. Part of me is itching to sit down and keep practising, another part of me is too embarrassed. Someone's been listening. And they've heard me play a rhumba version of 'Happy Frog'. This is humiliating.

I ring Zoë.

Thank God you called. Guess what I just found in the dictionary? There's a phrase in there called "Creeping Jesus". That's an actual phrase in the dictionary.

'What?'

Creeping Jesus. It's someone who's a fawning person. Which, personally, I think is a bit rough. Since when is Jesus associated with creepiness? Sure, he hung out with lepers – but that's not creepy. Social suicide maybe ...

'ZOE, SHUT UP. Listen to me for a second. You know how I've been trying to learn 'Jessica's Theme'? Well someone else is playing it. One of the neighbours has been listening to me practise 'Jessica's Theme' and now they're imitating me.'

Imagine next time someone's following you around and won't leave you alone, you can say, 'Fuck off Nadine, you are such a Creeping Jesus'.

'What? Who's Nadine?'

Well, no-one. That was just an example.

'Zoë, please.'

Fiiine. Spotlight back on you. So, someone is impersonating you? I'll put my money on the crying chick from next door. Margaret. It's obviously Margaret reaching out to you through music. Margaret's SOS from her I've-just-been-dumped-by-my-husband life.

'You really think it's Margaret?'

Sure. This is how these obsessions start. First it's the piano, next you notice some of your washing is going missing off the line ... she's just moments from taking on Jennifer Jason Leigh's role in Single White Female II, The Later Years. *You'll bump into her at Woolies and she'll be wearing one of your dresses and she'll have a maniacal look in her eye like Edward Norton in* Final Analysis *and she'll say "Hello, I'm Rachel Hill." And you'll say, "But I'M Rachel Hill" and she'll say, "No, I AM!" And that's when you get to say, Fuck off Margaret, you are such a Creeping ...*

I hang up.

The answer of course is to ring Patricia. Patricia will know who lives around here. Patricia will know who has been playing the piano during the day. It's three am in London. I don't care. I am being stalked by a piano-playing neighbour.

Patricia is of no help. Even taking into account that it's three am and she's a little groggy, she's still useless. All I find out from her is that Margaret lives at number forty-three. Which I suppose, considering my bedroom is at the back of the house, explains why I have gone to bed so many times listening to her cry. And no, Patricia does not remember Margaret having a piano, nor does she suspect that Margaret has the inclination to play 1980s movie theme songs. *Kramer vs. Kramer* maybe. But *The Man From Snowy River?* Not likely.

As for the other neighbours, Patricia sheepishly admits that she's not overly cluey on who lives on the other side at number forty-five nor who lives at the back of us. She thinks the house at forty-five is being rented by a young nurse who is never there during the day. I rule her out. And the house at the back used to be owned by a retired couple whose grown-up children would come and go at different times. But she thinks they might have moved out a few months ago. Does she recall hearing much piano music? Well, occasionally, but she's never paid that much attention to it. Does she know which house it might have come from? Well … no. Have I reconsidered entering Miss Brisbane?

Good night, Patricia.

There is nothing left to do but ring each of my friends and gauge their opinions. Simone thinks I should call the police. Katie thinks it's a secret admirer. Ally thinks it's possibly someone who's lonely. Pen thinks it's a coincidence. Nicky thinks it's someone having a laugh and proceeds to tell me the story of when she was eleven and learning 'When The Saints Go Marching In' on the recorder and how one of the neighbours left a note in her family's letter box saying that her playing was driving them up the wall. I explain to Nicky that that story has nothing to do with someone impersonating me on the piano and she just laughs and says she has to get back to work.

None of them except Simone seems overly worried. In fact, they are all more concerned about the Phil Collins 'No Jacket Required' songs that are playing in the background during these calls. I am forced to admit that I gave the tape an eleventh-hour stay of execution.

It's 1.45pm and I've gone from being a little freaked out and embarrassed to being annoyed. My friend the Piano Stalker is not going to stop me from practising dammit. Absolutely not. I shut all the curtains and the windows, sit back down at the piano and practise with the volume turned down low and Phil turned up high. Really high. Higher than Phil should ever been played.

And I wonder if tomorrow morning I will wake up to hear Piano Stalker doing its own musak version of 'Su-su-ssudio'.

Zoë picks me up at 5.20pm. She says that I am not allowed to mention the Piano Stalker for the rest of the evening. I spend the next seven minutes sulking, thinking about Piano Stalker in my mind. Just to spite her.

I saw Greg Windsor in Coles at Toowong Village yesterday, says Zoë as we trawl through Indooroopilly Shoppingtown looking for a park. *We ran into each other in the frozen food section.*

'Did you?' I say.

Yes. I forget, you dated him once didn't you? she says.

Zoë has not forgotten whether or not I once went on a date with Greg Windsor. Zoë is just being a bitch. Zoë wants me to once again say out loud what happened when I got to go on a date with my primary school boyfriend. I'm not playing this game today.

'I'm not playing this game today,' I say.

Why? What happened? pipes up a voice from the backseat.

Shit. Megan's in the car. Megan, Zoë's sixteen-year-old little sister who wanted to go late night shopping, while we went to the book signing.

Well, says Zoë. *It was like this …*

'I'll tell it. Greg Windsor was the boy that I had a crush on in primary school. And …'

And she always thought that he was "the one".

'I did not always think that he was "the one".'

Sure you didn't. Just every time after lectures at uni, when we used to go out drinking at the RE, Rachel would get drunk and start crying about how Greg Windsor was the only boy who ever loved her and how he used to type her name into the Space Invaders at the Captain Convenience Store on Moggill Road when he clocked the best score. And then you'd always go up to the jukebox in the RE beer garden and put on something by Pat Benatar and start wailing.

' "Love is a Battlefield" is a great song. Anyway,' I say, 'I ran into him at a party in 1996, he's a physio now and …'

Was he good looking? interrupts Megan.

'Divine-looking. Just gorgeous. Anyway he asked me out on a date. But it didn't work out.'

What happened? asks Megan suspiciously.

'Well, I agreed to meet him at the downstairs bar at Dooley's in the Valley. And when I got there I could see him at the bar. So I walked up to him and he gave me a kiss and told me I looked beautiful.'

Well, that sounds nice, says Megan.

Dear, sweet, naïve Megan.

Yeah, just wait for it, says Zoë.

'And then the bartender asked us what we'd like to drink. I asked for a vodka and lemonade. And …'

And?

'I ordered myself a vodka and lemonade and Greg ordered himself a West Coast Cooler.'

There's silence in the car.

'You understand what I'm saying, right? He ordered himself a *girlie drink*. I mean, I tried to pretend that it didn't matter but the whole time he was talking to me I just kept staring at the Westcoast Cooler with its perky tropical holiday label, thinking, "I can't date a guy who drinks girlie drinks". And I wanted to say, "Whoa, whoa, hold it right there buddy. What do you think you're doing?" I mean, a Stoli, Two Dogs, a Sub Zero I could have handled but a West Coast Cooler for fuck's sake? The only people who are allowed to order West Coast Coolers are seventeen-year-old girls. I can't date a guy who drinks that. I wanted to scream at him, "Order a beer for Christ's sake you big girl's blouse".'

I notice that I am yelling. I compose myself.

There is nothing to be said. Which is naturally Zoë's cue to speak.

Yet another reason to be a lesbian, she says in a matter-of-fact way, as if it's the obvious solution for Megan and myself. I've quickly learnt that Zoë is like an overzealous Christian: she's always out to recruit numbers.

'So how was Greg when you saw him?' I turn to Zoë wanting the full details.

Married. He was with his wife and their six-month-old baby. He was asking how you were and he said that he'd love to catch up with you and that they've just moved into a new house in Ascot. He said that he'd send us an invitation to their housewarming.

My heart sinks. Serves me right for being so shallow, I suppose.

'What did his wife look like?' I ask.

Nicole Kidman.

My face must visibly drop at this point, because Zoë quickly adds, *Hello? Nicole Kidman in* BMX Bandits.

'Liar.'

I laugh. Zoë laughs. Megan points out that we're about to hit a post.

We reverse park and arrange to meet Megan back at the car at nine pm.

By the time we get to the bookstore it's 5.40pm. A small crowd has already formed. There is a table set up near the New Releases section and I can see Dave Howard standing further back near the counter talking to a woman in a red suit with blonde hair. He has his back to us and he's wearing a grey Mooks shirt and black jeans. I remember seeing him on *Brisbane Extra* and him saying that his wardrobe consisted mainly of jeans and old t-shirts.

Twenty minutes later he's sitting at the table, signing books and making a lot of people laugh. There's a lot of laughter coming from the front of the queue. My palms get sweaty and the nerves kick in. Dave Howard is my favourite local author. And he's less than five metres away. I try to remain calm. Poised. Non-hysterical. I've got to play it cool.

'What are you going to say to him?' I ask Zoë.

What? I don't know. How about, 'It's Zoë, spelt Z. O. E …'

'We've got like a minute to a minute and a half to make an impression. We've got to say something witty. So he'll remember us.'

Yeah. And then he'll think we're so funny, he'll want to keep talking to us and he'll think "these are the type of people I would choose as friends". And he'll ask us to come back after the signing. And he'll invite us over to his house for dinner. And we'll become best friends with him. And …

She looks at me with her "Do you see how dumb you sound?" face.

'Fine.'

Zoë walks out of the queue and over to the Bargain Bin and starts picking up books. Her *laissez-faire* attitude is making me more nervous.

'Zee, get back over here,' I snap. 'There's only three people left in front of us. It's nearly our turn.'

And then it is. Zoë and I walk up to the desk.

Hi, says Dave Howard, smiling up at us from the table.

Hi, smiles Zoë. She looks over at me. I'm frozen with fear. She gives me a nudge. But I can't speak. So I smile. A closed mouth smile. The type of closed-mouth smile that belongs on the face of an insane, mute person. I look at Zoë in desperation.

So Zoë starts dishing out the Zoë Budd charm.

She mentions how she worked as a high school teacher before becoming a travel agent. She says how Dave's first young adult book *Amaze* was always a favourite of the kids. She says something witty. He laughs. He says something witty. She laughs. He scribbles something inside her book. They both laugh. And then they turn and look at me. The mute sidekick.

Are you an ex-teacher too? asks Dave Howard, looking up at me. Am I imagining it, or does he say this really slowly, mouthing the words clearly, as if I might be his first insane, mute fan who enjoys lip reading.

Minute and a half. Minute and a half. Bond with him. Bond with him dammit.

Finally I speak.

'No, I'm not a teacher, I'm a nanny. But I'm really great with kids. I'm like the Pied Piper,' I blurt out.

God, I'm a dick.

Right, says Dave Howard, a wry smile creeping over his lips. *The Pied Piper. Setting aside the possibility that he might have taken those kids away and murdered them, I guess.*

Zoë laughs out loud. I feel my face heating up.
'Well, I …'

Or the other explanation about them being killed somewhere on the way to the Children's Crusade.

'Um …'

No, I'm sure you're a very nice Pied Piper really. None of those creepy hidden agendas.

The blonde woman in the red suit comes over to the table.

Would you like a glass of water? she says.

'God I'd love one,' I concede with relief, which quickly turns to horror as Dave Howard simultaneously tells the woman, Sandra, that someone's already fetching him one.

Dave Howard turns and looks at me. Sandra looks at me, her carefully plucked eyebrows raised. Zoë is doubled over laughing.

'God, sorry. God, I'm so sorry. I just thought that she was ... I just thought for a second that ...'

I notice Sandra give Dave Howard the "is she a problem for you because we could have her taken out the back and dealt with" look. Dave Howard smiles back at her as if to say, "She's a harmless, insane fan who likes water. No problems here".

Dave Howard looks back at me. I am still yabbering some sort of apology about water and the Pied Piper and serial killers and how nervous I am to be meeting him.

It's fine. It's totally fine. We might make that two glasses of water, Sandra, and perhaps a chair. So who do I make this book out to? He looks up at me, smiling. I think he is finding this whole sequence of events a trifle amusing.

'Um, it's Rachel. Hill. Rachel Hill.'

Breathe. Breathe. Calm down.

'If you could just sign it *To Rachel.*'

Rachel the Pied-Piper, he says.

'Rachel the writer,' I say.

Rachel the nutter, we both think.

Okay, he says. *That's great.* He scribbles something onto the inside cover and hands it back to me. *There you go. Thanks for coming Rachel Hill.*

He sounds sincere.

I just stand there in front of him. Sandra returns with a chair and a glass of water but she's a little too late. My time is up.

He looks up at me and smiles again.

I smile back.

He smiles.

Zoë takes my arm and leads me away. And it's not until we're up at the food court that it dawns on me.

I met *Dave Howard*. I *met* Dave Howard. *I* met Dave Howard.

And I likened myself to a child-killer. Fuck. That's not the interaction I was hoping for. I don't envisage a dinner invite heading my way anytime soon.

I open up *August Moon* to see what he wrote inside.

Rachel
Next up: the real Ring A-Ring A-Rosie — a story of pestilence and death.
Stay great with those kids Pied Piper.
And good luck with the writing.
Dave Howard

9

When I get to Alex's house on Friday morning, I find her asleep in bed dressed in her ballet leotard and with a face full of glitter. Sharon has left me a note, asking if I would put on a load of washing before I leave and de-glitter her daughter before school.

I groan. Could there be a more difficult task than scrubbing the face of a six-year-old child?

Yes, apparently.

Because right on cue Snowy sashays past, looking like he's had a hard night out at the Sydney Mardi Gras. He is a walking disco ball. Alex has covered Snowy in glitter. She's tied a pink feather boa around his neck. There is tinsel around his tail. But worst of all, it would appear that Alex has painted Snowy's toenails Midnight Fuchsia. Yesterday

Snowy's biggest problem was that he had a wussy name. Twenty-four hours later and the word 'outed' springs to mind.

Snowy shimmies up to the bed and looks at me and then at his sleeping tormentor and then back at me, with a face that pleads 'Let's vote her off the island'. I explain to Snowy once again that I am in no mood for alliances. 'You have been watching too much *Survivor*', I say. He shimmies away. He leaves a trail of glitter in his wake. I make a mental note never to introduce Alex to the Bedazzler.

Then Alex wakes up. She stares at me and says, *Where's Mummy?*

'She just left for work.'

Alex sighs really loudly, like an old person whose joints ache.

Snowy hates you, she says matter-of-factly, the glitter crinkling around her eyes as she watches for my reaction.

'No, Snowy hates *The Boy From Oz* cast for creating a sequin-shortage in Australia.'

I laugh at my own joke. Alex glares at me.

'C'mon kiddo,' I say, scooping her up and throwing her over my shoulder in a fireman's carry. 'Let's go get some breakfast.'

In the car on the way home a song by Pearl Jam comes on the radio. It makes me think of Troy. I could turn the radio off, start humming a different tune, but I don't want to. This morning I want to be sad, just for a while. I listen. It's 'Better Man' – one of Troy's favourites. If he were here right now he'd have the radio turned up full blast and he'd be singing along, not caring who was listening. It used to bug him that I was never much of a Pearl Jam fan and he used to pester me constantly about them. We even had this running joke that if we got married I'd promise to 'love, honour and attend Pearl Jam concerts with him till death us do part'. We used to say that all the time and I'd pretend to protest and say that, in-turn, he would have to agree to do the Hungry Jacks run whenever I was hung-over. But on the day, inside the chapel, none of those things were ever said. Instead, I said the textbook vows with my fingers crossed behind my back.

By the time I get home, I go back to stressing about the Piano Stalker. I try to put it out of my mind. I continue to practise. The volume on the electric piano is still turned down low and this time, for a change, my *Xanadu* soundtrack is on full blast.

That'll teach 'em. I practise 'Jessica's Theme' for two hours. I'm still not getting any better. I decide to check the mail to see if my Tai-Bo tapes or Hairdini have arrived. And there it is. On the doorstep. At first, I stare at it and try to recall ringing and ordering piano accessories from Danoz Direct.

On my doorstep sits a large, brand new metronome with a pink ribbon tied around it. It hasn't been posted. It has been "dropped off". I pick it up. I look around. I wonder how long it has been sitting there.

I take it inside and offer it a seat at the kitchen bench. There must be some mistake. I pick it up again and study it and that's when I notice that a note has been sticky-taped to the bottom. I unfold it. In rather scrawly handwriting it says:

> Don't be put off. I'd much rather listen to you practise than Phil Collins or *Xanadu*. Some advice ... the piece is meant to be played legato. Slow it down and it'll sound a lot better.

I'm beginning to get a little freaked out again. I study the note. It's been written in black pen. The handwriting is messy. I debate what is worse. The fact that Piano Stalker is now sending me gifts or that Piano Stalker is critiquing my playing like a judge on *Star Search*. I read over the note and that's when I realise that I can see type on the other side of the paper. I turn it over and notice that this note has in fact been written on the back of an old email. An email to SQ1437@uq.edu.au from the University of Queensland's Email Account Service. Apparently, SQ1437's account size is over the limit. SQ1437 needs to delete some files.

And I wonder if this is who has been listening to me play. This SQ1437.

10

I ring Zoë to tell her about the mystery gift. She comes straight over.

'I thought you were working today?'

Yeah, I was. But I told them that you rang threatening to kill yourself. So they let me leave early. She stuffs some almond bread into her mouth and hoists herself up onto the kitchen bench. *Oh and Rach,* she says with her mouth full, *I'm obliged to tell you that suicide is not the answer. It's not.*

'I'm not planning on committing suicide.'

Well sure. Not yet. But let's face it, your life's pretty fucked.

She grins at me.

I get out the metronome and show her the note. 'Who do you think it is?'

Miss Scarlett. In the drawing room. With the lead piping.

'Be serious. Do you still think it's Margaret?'

Of course it's not Margaret. I was only telling you that stuff the other night to mess with your head. She studies the metronome, examining it carefully. *Christ, as soon as your life looks like it's become as shitty as everyone else's this kinda thing happens to you. You know who it'll be? It'll be some gorgeous guy who lives around here who's fallen in love with your piano playing. It'll be your bloody soulmate, someone who's too shy to come and talk to you face to face. So stop stressing. You've got nothing to lose. Just email him.*

'Zoë, we don't know it's a *he*.'

Oh please. As if it's not a guy … She jumps down from the kitchen bench. *I'm going. This time call me before you get married – I'd like to be there next time you say "Sure, I'll give it another burl".*

And with that she leaves me alone with the metronome and the note. I'm still totally unsure of how to handle this but then, as Zoë said, "What have I got to lose?"

So I go to my computer and get online.

Subject: Thank you for the metronome
Date: Friday 1.18pm
From: RachelHill@mymail.com.au
To: SQ1437@uq.edu.au

Dear SQ1437@uq.edu.au
Thank you for the metronome. I will try to keep the noise level down from now on.
Sincerely
Rachel Hill

I press send. I go and make myself a coffee. Sharon rings.

She's caught up at the studio and she doesn't think that she'll be able to make the three o'clock bell. Do I think that I might be able to pick Alex up and then take her to her ballet lesson at Kenmore Village?

'Sure thing,' I say. I like Sharon. She looks a little like Sharon Stone in some ways. Cropped sandy blonde hair, small face with high cheekbones. And a nose that has been seasoned with freckles. I think she's about thirty-three but looks older. Or maybe just more tired than a thirty-three-year-old should look. Sharon works full time as a vision switcher at Channel Seven. She arranges her roster so that the vision she is switching is more *Sunrise* and *Humphrey B Bear* rather than any programs that appear after three pm. But some days it doesn't always work out that way. Sometimes she has to stay back or cover someone else's shift.

I barely see her in the mornings. I usually arrive and Sharon is running out the door and into her beat-up Mitsubishi Colt. It's funny, baby-sitting and being in a stranger's house. It's funny that you know so little about them but you get to walk around their life, like a tourist wondering through the Pompeii ruins judging someone else's existence without knowing who they really are. I see Sharon's hairbrush in the bathroom; I know that she buys cheap shampoo but expensive deodorant; I know that she rinses her cereal bowl every morning but can't be bothered to stack it into the dishwasher. I know she likes reading books on art, owns far too many Spandau Ballet records and dabbles in painting, but I don't know who Alex's father is, whether Sharon was ever married or how long it's been just the two of them.

At first, it used to bug me that Alex was allowed to stay up so late at night. And that I would regularly find her curled up under a doona in yesterday's clothes rather than her nightie. But I have quickly learnt Sharon does her best. And she loves Alex more than anything.

I decide to pick up a new packet of Froot Loops on my way to Kenmore Hills State School. It's only 2.30pm, still half an hour until Alex is let loose from Mrs Healy's classroom. I walk into Woolworths at Kenmore. As I go through the turnstile I pick up a basket, just in case I see any other items that look worthy of purchasing. Near the baskets are maps. I have never noticed these before. Maps of Woolworths. How strange. It's the layout of the store, indicating what items can be found in each aisle. This is brilliant, I think. This is an organised, streamlined, controlled way to shop. I take a map with me and vow to use it in future. This map is part of the new Rachel Hill. Rachel Hill, the achiever. Rachel Hill, shopper with a map.

Ten minutes later, I am sitting in the car outside Alex's primary school listening to the radio and waiting for the bell. Waiting for the stampede of green shirts and checked dresses to come storming out of classrooms. And there it goes. For a child under twelve, the three o'clock bell must be the happiest sound in the world, after Mr Whippy's xylophone version of 'Greensleeves'. And then I see Alex, skipping along holding hands with her friend, Emma. I get out of the car and wave but as soon as she sees me she freezes.

And then Alex starts to limp. Her happy smile becomes a grimace and she begins hobbling towards me. If I hadn't already seen her skipping with Emma, it would be quite convincing. Except for the part where the limp changes sides.

'Hello Banana-Brain.'

Where's Mum?

'She's still at the studio, so I'm here to take you to ballet.'

Oh, she says, putting on her sad face to match her sad voice. *Rachel, I don't think I can go to ballet. I hurt my leg. Did you see me? I can't really walk. Can Emma come over to play?*

'But you were just skipping. You came out of your classroom skipping with Emma.'

Well, Emma kicked me.

'Emma kicked you?'

Yes.

'Why would Emma do that?'

She kicks everyone.

'U-huh. Which leg hurts?'

She thinks about this for a moment and then points to her left leg and says *Both.*

'Okay, look Alex, your mum told me that you have a ballet concert coming up and that you can't really miss any classes. So I think you'll have to go. If your legs hurt you can just sit in the corner of the studio and watch the others. Emma can come over another day.'

FINE! she says stomping up to the car, the limp disappearing faster than Sofie Formica.

'How was school?' I ask, as she puts on her seatbelt.

For the sixth time, it was BAD! she yells at me, staring down at her lap before becoming intrigued by an old pink hair clip lying on the car floor.

'You don't have to yell at me,' I say, before tentatively asking her what happened.

Lucy Watson took something what wasn't hers and then blamed it on me.

'Bugger,' I say. And we drive home in silence. Me contemplating what it was that Lucy took. And Alex wondering what a pink hair clip would look like on Snowy's head.

11

I think I'd do lip-syncing. To 'We Didn't Start The Fire' by Billy Joel. It's a hard song. Lots of tricky lyrics about Red China and Walter Winchell and Doris Day and punk rock. Anyone can mouth the words to 'Oh What A Night'. Few people can pull off 'We Didn't Start The Fire' and still put in the emotion. Make it convincing. Have you believing in the fire.

But of course there isn't a talent section. Not in Miss Brisbane. And the whole reason I'm driving into the city this morning is to un-register myself. So even if there was a talent section, even if they said to me, 'Rachel, you'd like to lip-sync wouldn't you? Any song of your choice, Rachel. All you have to do is stay registered', I'd still put my foot down. I'd say no. No, I will not lip-sync for you. No, I do not want to be in this pageant. Even though I know that I could clean up with my 'We Didn't Start The Fire.' Even though I know that the tiara and the cloak and the sceptre would be mine.

I automatically turn down Turbot Street, as if I'm going to my old work place, the *Escape* offices. But this is not where I need to be. I need to be on George Street.

I need to find a carpark on George Street. My mobile phone beeps. It's an SMS message from Zoë that says *SMS me back as soon as you've quit. Don't make me come down there and do it for you.*

I'm not feeling upbeat. Not as upbeat as someone should feel when they are about to collect a $150 refund. I pull up at the lights outside the Palace Backpackers. I conveniently forget about the $91 already spent on magazines and try to imagine what I could do with $150. Eat a shitload of mayo, that's what I could do. I say this out loud. Out loud, as if the question was asked by Eddie McGuire and you're allowed to say "shitload" on *Who Wants To Be A Millionaire*. I look left and see that the guy in the car beside me is staring at me. I pretend that I was humming. Not talking out loud to myself. I nod my head up and down and hum a bit. I think I look unconvincing. This is what my life has become. Pretending to hum at traffic lights on my way to a Miss Brisbane meeting where I want to get $150 to spend on mayo.

By the time I find 257 George Street, I'm fifteen minutes late. I'm feeling nervous. But that's stupid. No need to feel nervous. I'm just going to walk in, explain that there has been a mistake, collect the money and leave. No fuss. No-one's upset. This is not a problem. A problem would be if they said that refunds weren't given. That Patricia had signed a contract. That they would take me to court if I refused to compete ... or if I had lied about my marital status. And then I'd be forced, FORCED to take my story to *A Current Affair,* who would be on my side and want to film lots of footage of me gazing forlornly at Patricia's Miss Goulbourn sash and then do close-ups of me standing outside the Miss Brisbane offices gazing wistfully at the door before looking in my empty purse.

I push the glass door open and walk up to the middle-aged woman standing behind a desk that, I gather, was once covered in nametags. It looks like Liz Williams and I are the only ones left to arrive. The woman behind the desk says her name is Jan. She has shoulder-length red hair and is wearing rather enormous gold earrings and an over-sized cotton T-shirt that has a glittery puff-paint cockatoo on the front. She has a fat belt slung over the top of the shirt. I hate her.

Hello there. Rachel or Liz?

'Rachel Hill.'

She goes on to introduce herself as Jan Kingsley – née Ramsden. Miss Port-Pirie 1973. Jan hands me a plastic bag that appears to be full of brochures and booklets. She says that she works with Fergus and is a bit of a Mother Hen to the girls and that she's glad I made it to the meeting. She hands me a name tag. I tell her that I can't stay long and that I'd prefer not to wear it. She looks at me. I pin it on. Jan's got a formidable "don't fuck with me" stare working for her. Whoever Liz Williams is, I am beginning to wish I was with her.

Jan tells me to walk on through and meet the other girls. I tell her that I am here to get a registration fee refund. She purses her lips. She tilts her head to the side. She tells me that I will need to see Fergus. And then she turns her back on me and starts stuffing envelopes.

I walk past reception and into the main room. I can't see this Fergus character anywhere. I look around. There are about thirty girls in the room. They are X-rays with lipstick. I drink five glasses of punch in ten minutes, pushing the reasonable boundaries of bladder capacity. I go to find the ladies toilet.

Ten minutes later and I'm doing a circuit of the room, looking for Fergus McLaughlin. But he's nowhere in sight. In fact, I can't see any organisers anywhere. So now what am I supposed to do? I notice a girl sitting on a couch by the window filling in a form. I decide to go and sit next to her. If I have to wait around for Fergus, I may as well be comfortable.

I make my way over to the lounge and sit next to a girl who is writing so much that she's had to use both sides of the sheet.

I try and look at what she's writing. But I can't quite read it. I lean in a little closer. She looks up at me.

Do you want one? And she grabs another sheet and a pencil from the seat beside her and hands it to me. *We have to hand it in to Fergus before we leave. I think it's for media and stuff.*

'Thanks.' I glance over the sheet. 'Do you know where Fergus is?'

I think he's gone to pick up a few more fundraising booklets.

'Right.' I start to read over the sheet. The beginning part is standard name, date of birth, address and phone number. The next section is a little trickier. It's all about likes and dislikes, goals, ambitions, favourite hobbies and skills.

The girl next to me has turned her sheet back over and is now re-reading her answers. I let my eyes slide over to her sheet and try hard to decipher her handwriting. Shit, she's written down that she's fluent in Cantonese, Mandarin and German.

She looks up at me.

I quickly turn my head and pretend to be reading over my own sheet.

She turns back.

My eyes slide over to her sheet again. She won a Nescafé Big Break Award when she was eighteen for designing her own brand of moisturiser. And she's studying Commerce/Law. I read down to her goals section. I lean in a little closer. She wants to sail around the ... I can't quite make out the next bit ... I lean in just a little more ... Young Endeavour so that she can ... I can't read that next word ... just a little closer ... and then ...

I feel a hand on my shoulder.

Rachel? I just spoke to Fergus on his mobile and the good news is that he told me I could handle your refund, says Jan.

'Oh, great. That's really great.' I feel relieved. And then

suddenly the girl who was sitting next to me is gone and Jan is beside me. She takes my hand in hers.

The bad news Rachel, I'm afraid, is that I'm just not going to let you quit this award.

I smile weakly, not quite sure what's going on.

I've read your file Rachel. You are exactly the type of girl we're looking for.

'Look, Jan, I appreciate what you're saying but this really isn't ...'

I know that you used to be the Features Editor of a big travel magazine. And your mother told us that before that you spent a number of years working in Public Relations, organising publicity and events and sponsorship. You are exactly the type of woman who could make a difference in this award. You have such a good chance at winning this. A lot of these girls have never organised a fundraising event before. They don't know the first thing about getting publicity for themselves. How to sell tickets. Get attention.

'Yeah, sure, but I'm sorry I just really can't be in this. You've got a fundraising booklet which I'm sure explains how to do everything. So you know, I'm sorry I just ...'

Are you sure I can't change your mind? I could use someone like you, that's all. You're the type of entrant we're trying to attract.

'That's really kind of you but ...'

Alright, alright, your mind is obviously made up – which is a shame. But umm, she pauses and looks at the fundraising booklet she has in her hand. *Well, our Marketing Officer resigned a few months back, and we haven't had a chance to replace her. So, while you're here, it would be great if you could give the girls some tips on getting publicity. You know, tell them how they should* approach the media. Maybe throw in a few tips on organising an event? I mean, I would really appreciate it. And then I'll organise your refund and I won't hassle you.*

'Um, okay. I just can't stay for too long. I need to get back home to …'

Oh Rachel Williams, she says putting her arm around my shoulders.

'It's um Hill. Rachel Hill.'

Of course it is, love. She gives my shoulders a squeeze. *This will be great. Look, here's our fundraising booklet. It's a bit out of date but it has a few tips for the girls — so maybe have a quick look over that. And then, what if I get you to talk to the girls in twenty minutes? Would that be alright?*

'Sure,' I say, which is polite-girl talk for "I'm only agreeing to this because I want my refund".

I watch Jan wander off and I am left on the couch with a red pen and a suspiciously thin "How to Fundraise" booklet. I can't believe I've been roped into this. Talk about getting her pound of flesh out of me before I leave.

Twenty minutes later and I am still sitting on the couch and the booklet is covered in red pen. Not only is this book badly written but the ideas are archaic. Jan and Fergus are recommending activities like raffles and lamington drives and car washes – which are all well and good but will raise the entrants hardly any money. The media contact list is completely out of date. And the media release template is awful — their sample lead sentence is so bad that an editor would just throw the release out. I can't help myself. I write corrections and suggestions all over the booklet. If entrants follow this booklet this award really will be in trouble. I look at my watch and try to collect my thoughts. And then Jan signals to me that we're about to begin.

Ladies, I'd like to have your attention for a moment. We're very lucky to have Rachel Hill here. Rachel is a former Features Editor and she also has a background in PR and Marketing. So Rachel has kindly agreed to give us all some tips on organising events and also on how to deal with the media. Let's give her a round of applause.

And then I'm on. I take the microphone from Jan and she hands me a pen for the white board behind me.

One hour later and I'm still fielding questions from the group. So far we've covered the basics in organising publicity, how to write a media release, how to get the media to attend an event, interview tips and techniques and some sure-fire fundraising events that I learnt from Zoë and Patricia over the years.

The entrants themselves have completely surprised me. Are they thin? Sure. Do they all look like they've gone to deportment classes? Yep. But are they bimbos? Nowhere near it. Instead, they ask intelligent, thoughtful questions. It becomes pretty clear that the majority of girls who have entered the Miss Brisbane Awards are doing so for reasons other than tiaras and cloaks. Most of them seem to have a personal connection to the charities they are raising funds for. At least two thirds of the group has mothers or brothers or friends or uncles who have been helped by the Salvos or the Red Cross or the Leukemia Foundation or the Cancer Fund. Others just seem to want to do something that makes a difference to the community – as clichéd as that sounds. And I can't help but admire them for that. And I can't help but want to be a part of it. Because hearing them talk about raising money to buy new equipment in the children's cancer wards or to fund the soup van for another year at City Mission ... well it just makes you want to get involved. Pitch in. Because that kind of stuff seems important. More important than me sitting on my arse watching telly.

On top of that, I gotta admit that I'm feeling pretty good up here. With an audience. I'd forgotten what this feels like – running something. Organising people. Feeling knowledgeable and on top of things. Feeling useful.

Simone from Keperra interrupts my thoughts.

Rachel, do you still work on the magazines?

'Ah, no. These days I'm working part-time, well freelance really. From home.'

Simone rolls her eyes jokingly and says, *Half your luck, you'll have so much time to fundraise.*

I am too embarrassed to tell them the truth. That I am pulling out.

As we're wrapping up the session, someone else calls out *Jan, is all of this information Rachel's just given us available in a booklet or anything?*

I shrug my shoulders apologetically. Jan steps in and says *No, it's not. But perhaps you girls can share notes.*

Without thinking it through, I find myself telling the group that I will type up the information I have just given them and email it to Jan over the weekend. And then I tell them that I will include my contact details and that they can email or phone me if they want me to help them with their media releases.

Jan turns to me and whispers *Rachel, you know you could stay registered and if – down the track – you wanted to quit, you still could. But it would be a shame not to have you involved. You're really good at this.*

I find myself saying okay. Okay, I'll stay. Because I can quit this award down the track. But right now, I'm needed.

12

I am still buzzing when I get home from the meeting. This awards thing is great. Even if I don't raise any money myself, I can help these other girls. And then pull out. That's fine. Not a problem. I feel good about myself again. Like the old me.

I can't help but laugh that despite years of protests, I have ended up entering a pageant. I go to the mirror and take a long, hard look at myself. Just to see if I'm Miss Brisbane material.

I suck my cheeks in. I pile my hair on top of my head. Caitlin would laugh so hard if she knew that I entered this. We always had a pact that neither of us would give in to Patricia's pestering. And out of the two of us, Caitlin was the one who really was "Beauty Queen" material. Not me. In our household, I was the smart one and Caitlin was the pretty one. Caitlin was the one who had a constant stream of boyfriends. Caitlin was the one who had a part-time job at Splendiferous while I was shovelling fries in my polyester Hungry Jacks uniform. Caitlin was the one who got asked to her first Formal when she was still in Year Ten. I only ever went to one Formal, my Year Twelve one, and even then I had to take Cameron, the son of someone in Patricia's tennis group. It didn't help that Caitlin was sitting two tables away. She was our School Captain's date.

I dig out a photo of me taken before I left for the formal. I cringe at my 80s hair. I cringe at the dress I'm wearing - a big taffeta, strapless number with lots of tulle. I look like I've walked straight out of the 'Girls Just Wanna Have Fun' filmclip. But that aside, I do look kinda cute. And slim.

I have no choice. I'm going to have to get that dress out from the back of the cupboard and see if it still fits me.

It does.

If I don't pull the zip all the way up.

I put on some music and get out my makeup bag. I look in the mirror again. I start to re-do my makeup. Just a little.

By the time the tape ends, I've put on so much makeup that I look like a hooker. An 80s hooker. I am the poor man's Pretty Woman.

I find an old banana-clip and pull my hair back off my face and then I hairspray my hair, like it has never been hairsprayed before, emptying an entire can of Wella Super Hold on my head. My hair is now rock hard. It could double as a bike helmet. I survey myself in the full-length mirror. Shoes. I need shoes. I find a pair of Caitlin's stilettos.

I put on some Hall and Oates, do my best *Young Talent Time* dancing and lip-sync in the mirror to 'She's A Man-Eater'. I pose for imaginary social pages photos. Me, the new Miss Brisbane, with a glass of champagne in my hand posing with my judges. I slink around my bedroom. I slink past the metronome with the big pink ribbon that is still sitting on my bookcase. I stop slinking. Suddenly I remember SQ1437 and the email that I sent. I wonder if they've answered? I wobble my way down to the study to find out.

I log on. I have one new message. It's from somebody called Matthew Harding. It was sent last night. Shit.

> Subject: Re: Thank you for the metronome
> Date: Friday 11.27pm
> From: Matthew Harding <USQ1437@uq.edu.au
> To: RachelHill@mymail.com.au
>
> Rachel
> You don't have to keep the noise down. I enjoy listening to you practise, it breaks the monotony of my day. But if I have to listen to you playing eighties music, can I at least make a request?
> Matt :)

Without thinking much about it, I email him back.

> Subject: Re Re: Thank you for the metronome
> Date: Saturday 2.25pm
> From: RachelHill@mymail.com.au
> To: SQ1437@uq.edu.au

Dear Matt
No.
Rachel Hill

I decide to write Caitlin an email and tell her that I am wearing her stilettos and that I am holding them hostage until she returns my jacket and CDs. I press send and then a message comes up. I have one new message. Shit. It would seem that SQ1437 a.k.a Matthew Harding is on-line right now.

> Subject: Re Re Re: Thank you for the metronome
> Date: Saturday 2.31pm
> From: Matthew Harding <USQ1437@uq.edu.au
> To: RachelHill@mymail.com.au
>
> Dear Ms Hill (this has become just so formal, hasn't it?)
> What's next, Huey Lewis and the News?
> Matt

I go into my bedroom and find my 'Hip To Be Square' cassingle. I put it in my stereo and play it really, really loud. I go back to the computer and scour the Internet for naked shots of Huey Lewis to send to Matt in another email. Another message comes up.

> Subject: Re Re Re: Thank you for the metronome
> Date: Saturday 2.34pm
> From: Matthew Harding <USQ1437@uq.edu.au
> To: RachelHill@mymail.com.au
>
> I bet you own a Mel and Kim cassette.

His email makes me laugh, but I'm feeling a little uneasy. I don't know anything about this guy. I wonder if he's creepy. I feel like I'm in one of those dodgy Internet chatrooms where people swap measurements and give themselves cyber-names like Hotlove and the guys who say they're twenty-three are actually forty-eight-year-old high school teachers who live at home with their parents. This is stupid. And dangerous. This should stop. Although he sounds like he could be my age. He doesn't sound creepy. This whole thing is ridiculous. It's like some kind of bad movie with Meg Ryan and Tom Hanks. Snap out of it Rachel. Goodbye Hollywood email liaison. Hello reality of him being a *Silence-of-the-Lambs*-style killer who seeks clothing made from my skin.

> Subject: Re Re Re Re: Thank you for the metronome
> Date: Sunday 2.42pm
> From: RachelHill@mymail.com.au
> To: <USQ1437@uq.edu.au
> Matt
> I appreciate your emails and the metronome but I am really not keen on having an email correspondence with someone that I don't know! For all I know you could be Hannibal Lecter!!!!
> Kind Regards
> Rachel Hill
> PS I'm only on-line at the moment because I am awaiting an email from my mother.

I debate the exclamation marks at the end. Too many? My logic is that the exclamation mark brings a light-hearted tone to the message. Just in case Matt is creepy, we don't wanna go pissing him off. We don't want him to think I've been rude. We want to keep him on-side, like they do with serial killers in *Law and Order*. But perhaps four is a bit much. Zoë hates the whole !!!! or worse still the !?! style of punctuation. She thinks that for every extra exclamation mark you use, you have to take ten points off your IQ. I decide to delete three of them and just leave one. So naturally I hit the send button by accident before I make any changes and my flock of exclamation marks are excitedly hurtling through cyber-space seconds later. Damn.

I stumble back upstairs in my boots and stand out on the veranda. I look around at the houses that surround me. Where is he? Where are you Matthew Harding? In other news, my banana clip is digging into my scalp.

I head back downstairs and realise that I have left my computer connected to the Internet, so I teeter over to turn it off. I wonder if Matthew Harding has emailed me back? I can't help but be a little curious. I go back into my In Box just to check his reaction to my swift departure. I have one message.

> Subject: Quid Pro Quo Clarice
> Date: Saturday 2.47pm
> From: Matthew Harding <USQ1437@uq.edu.au>
> To: RachelHill@mymail.com.au
>
> Rachel Hill wrote:
> For all I know you could be Hannibal Lecter!!!!

You're right!!!! We should meet!!!! Break out the Chianti, I'll be over in five minutes to introduce myself.
Matt.
PS So how's Mum? (see how familiar I am with you? Sweet, isn't it?)

My first thought is to think 'Bastard' for making an issue out of my, albeit excessive, exclamation mark usage. My second thought is to look at the clock. It's 2.51pm. This email was sent at 2.47pm. Matthew Harding will be here in one minute. Shit. I go upstairs. I pace around. I try to calm down. I decide that the sensible, mature thing is to just open the door. And I stick with that decision until I pass the hallway mirror and realise that I'm wearing gold elbow length fingerless gloves and blue eye shadow.

There's a knock on the door.

He's one minute early.

FUCK! He's here. He's here. Shit. **Option one** is that I could pretend I'm not home. But he knows that I'm home, 'cause I've been on the computer. **Option two** is to grab my packet of Froot Loops and ring Zoë.

You can't just leave him standing at the front door, she screeches when I tell her the story. *At least go and look through the peephole and see what he looks like.*

He knocks again.

'Coming!' I call out meekly with a mouthful of Loops. Phone to my ear I tiptoe up to the peephole to get a look at this SQ1437@uq.edu.au.

Well, says Zoë?

I look through the peephole. And I see him. Standing on

the doorstep, looking down at the ground with his hands in his pockets, is a twenty-something guy in bare feet wearing a rather grubby-looking pair of faded jeans and a They Might Be Giants T-shirt. He has a mop of thick scruffy brown hair and a medium build. More importantly, I see no weapons. Even more importantly, he's not wearing a hand-made patchwork skin waistcoat.

He knocks again.

Hello Rachel? It's Matt. Are you there? calls out an unfamiliar voice from the other side of my mahogany front door.

Well? says Zoë again. *At least tell me what he looks like.*

'Shhhh,' I say.

I can't answer the door looking like this. And I don't like the idea of him coming around here.

'Ahh, I can't really answer the door at the moment,' I say from the safety of my hallway. I sit down on the tiles. I don't feel well. I start to wonder if you can OD on Froot Loops. I should definitely post that letter to Kellogg's.

How come? calls out Matthew Harding.

'How come?' I say to Zoë.

Ahh, because you're sick, she whispers back.

'I'm sick,' I call out to Matt. And then I cough really loudly to make it more plausible, if only in my mind. And then I cough again and this time it's a little more real-sounding because I'm actually choking on a Froot Loop.

'I've got …'

Think of something, Rachel.

'… scurvy. And I'm not allowed to go near anyone for another few days.'

Scurvy? Where the fuck did that come from? Where were you, on the Endeavour? says Zoë. *So what does he look like?*

I start to tell her. I whisper about the old jeans, the T-shirt, the no-shoes and the medium build, in between mouthfuls of Froot Loops.

Yeah but what does he look like? pesters Zoë. *Is he good looking?*

'Yes. No. Oh, I don't know Zee. It's hard to tell. Does it matter?'

Hello? Yes it fucking matters. You're a disgrace to desperate straight chicks everywhere.

'This isn't Hollywood. I've looked through the peephole and you know what? Harry Connick Junior is not standing on the other side of my front door. It's just some ordinary guy.'

Hope Floats *sucked*, says Zoë.

'I know it sucked. This is not a debate about the suckiness of *Hope Floats*. I'm not saying …'

Your friend's right.

I look up.

Matthew is staring at me through the bay window next to the front door.

Hey, he says, nodding his head in acknowledgement of me. *Your friend is right, though.* Hope Floats *sucked.*

I'm like a rabbit caught in headlights. Frozen. Matt can see me in all my non-scurvy taffeta glory. It's not like I didn't know that there was a bay window next to the front door but who the fuck steps off the path and onto the tan bark to look through a window? This is not part of the rules. He has broken the rules.

'You're not supposed to step on the tan bark,' I yell. 'Who steps on the tan bark to look through the window? Nobody. No one. No one steps off the path. That's why there's a fucking path. You're supposed to stay on the path leading to the front door.'

I scramble to my feet, which is hard to do in stiletto heels – I stumble back onto my knees.

'Ow,' I say as if I am blaming him. 'Ow.'

Is this really about the tan bark thing or because you're dressed …

Zoë starts laughing. I hang up on her.

'Don't even say it. Don't even make a comment about what I'm wearing. What about you? What kind of neighbour spies on people through their windows? When clearly, clearly, there's a fucking pathway.'

Righto. I'm umm sorry. I wasn't aware. Of the tan bark/pathway rules. Look, I'm moving back. Off the tan bark and to the front door where I can't see you. See? he calls out from his front-door position, now out of sight. *I can't see you anymore. I'm back on the path.*

'Well, it's a bit late now, isn't it. I've already flashed my undies at you. So just go. Go away.' And I crawl off into the kitchen, Froot Loops crunching under my knees.

13

I need to get out of here. I call my friends Claire and Angus and invite them to the RE for some beer and Saturday night pool.

I need to relax. I am beginning to get tense. Why are these things happening to me? I've been home alone for one week and somehow I have managed to make my life a shitload worse than it already was. I've humiliated myself in front of Dave Howard. I'm still signed up to the Miss Brisbane Awards and I've got a neighbour who makes house-calls, who I reward with a quick flash of my undies. Excellent Rachel. Excellent. Good job. Way-to-fucking-go.

I've arranged to meet Angus and Claire in the beer garden at seven-ish. I've known Angus since uni and Claire has been his girlfriend for close to four years. They got engaged last month. They're great. I love them, but my newfound singleness irritates them. They liked Troy, they thought he was perfect for me and they're sorry we split up, but they feel it's time for me to move on. They're itching to set me up on a date. I'm not getting any younger, as Claire likes to remind me. She makes me feel like my eggs are minutes away from becoming 'snap-dried'.

They've already nabbed a table by the time I get there, which is pretty tricky for a Saturday night at the RE. We take turns at buying the drinks. We play a game of pool. Claire insists that she can't play, that she's a terrible player. She proves this by sinking the black within the first five minutes. And tearing a small hole in the felt. And then taking the two one-dollar coins on the rim of the table, chanting *Find a penny pick it up and all day long you'll have good luck.*

We catch up on each other's news. But tonight I'm feeling unsettled. Overly sensitive. Tonight, I cringe every time I see Claire brush Angus's fringe out of his eyes. I turn away when I notice Angus whispering a private joke into Claire's ear. Usually it doesn't bother me, especially not from these two. But tonight it grates on me. It's uncomfortable like an itchy wool sweater that you just want to take off. I don't know why but tonight, being at the RE, makes me feel lonely. Troy's shadow lingers.

I remember the last time he'd come to Brisbane. We'd gone to the RE with the gang to watch Women in Docs play and we'd gotten completely drunk. He was making everyone laugh and I was sitting on his lap and he was playing with my ponytail. He used to twist it around his fingers. And I was sitting there laughing about some stoned girl who was up dancing by herself in front of the band to the song 'Tin Roof'. And then I remember how Troy grabbed my hand and led me up to the space in front of the stage and started spinning me around. He was waltzing me around, really fast. And I remember that I kept stepping on his feet. And I remember laughing and laughing, until tears were in my eyes and my mascara started to smudge. And I remember that I was really happy that night. I was really, really happy.

I want to go home.

But then Angus says *Your shout Hill!* and I'm brought back to this evening, to this pub full of polo shirts and fob chains and grubby football jerseys and 'Khe Sahn'.

You alright? says Angus. I look into his face. We went out once. Just briefly when we were at uni. I've never noticed how big the gap is between his front teeth. I wonder if that's something Claire loves or loathes. Angus. He's worried about me. So I smile my best cheery smile, and say, 'Yes, of course you big idiot' and make my way to the bar, vowing to make a quick exit after I've had a glass of water and delivered the happy couple another two VBs.

I wait at the bar. I stare at the bar staff. Watch them. I wouldn't mind working in a bar, I think. I contemplate life behind the bar. The downfall of course is that, unlike being a writer, I would actually have to get out of my pyjamas to do the work. The blonde girl behind the bar asks me what I'd like and I put in my order for two pots of VB, a glass of water and my own flat in St Lucia with river views.

So I hope that's an orange juice you're ordering ... Scurvy Lady.

If I stand still and don't turn around perhaps I can pretend this isn't happening.

But the thing that isn't happening is now tapping me on the shoulder.

I turn around. It's Matt Harding. Wearing exactly what he had on this afternoon when he was standing on my doorstep. Plus shoes.

He looks at me and smiles. He has something in his teeth.

I stand there and stare at him. He looks about six foot three. His front tooth has a tiny chip in it. I'm disappointed to notice that he really does look nothing like Harry Connick Junior. In fact, he's a little ordinary. Less than ordinary. Pedestrian, even.

Hi, he says extending his hand. *I'm Matthew, Matt, your neighbour.*

'Sure,' I say, holding up the two pots of beer I ordered to explain why I can't respond to the handshake. I wonder what my chances are of ditching the beers and doing the old Harold Holt bolt.

I'll carry this one for you, he says, taking my glass of water.

'You've got something in your teeth,' I say, pointing out the piece of green wedged between his fangs.

Sure. Sure I do. I know that. I put it there deliberately as an icebreaker. Give us something to talk about. But now that it's served its purpose I should probably ditch it. Or maybe even save it for the next neighbour I try to befriend. I think it'll work a treat on Margaret at number 43.

'Does she play the piano too? Or is it just me that you're bugging?'

Triangle, actually. And scurvy's not a problem for her. She has leprosy issues. So, don't you go thinking you're special.

I find a smile creeping onto my face. Which annoys me, so I start to walk back to Angus and Claire. As I come into view Angus and Claire look up at me and smile. I roll my eyes and do my best 'don't ask' face as Matt comes up, puts my glass of water on the table and introduces himself to Claire and Angus as my next door neighbour. Their faces light up. Claire is practically dribbling with excitement. I am *so* not in the mood for this. They invite him to sit down.

I sit there and smile weakly as Matt explains to Angus and Claire how he's been listening to me practise 'Jessica's Theme'.

Why were you playing 'Jessica's Theme'? asks Claire, looking at me in wonder, all arched eyebrows and open-mouthed.

'I bet Zoë I could learn it before my birthday,' I say nonchalantly, lying through my teeth. I cross my arms. And then my legs. I set the alligators into the moat. My throat is dry. I am beginning to feel suffocated.

'And I didn't stop practising,' I add. 'I just turned the volume down.' But my voice has taken the form of skywriting. The letters fade a little, get separated and are lost amongst the swirl of my companion's beer-flavoured banter. No one seems to care what I have to say. It appears that Claire and Angus are honeymooning with our new table companion. He's making them laugh. Their bodies lean in towards him, like two hungry pups salivating over a butcher's bone. I'm not sure that I am even at this table. Perhaps I'm not. I tune out.

The words *Rachel's writing a book* drift past my ears. I tune back in. I hear *travel magazine features editor* and *parents' house* and *London*. Please stop. Please stop. Please stop. I turn away and study the face of the girl sitting at the table behind me. She looks a little like Helen Hunt. She looks up at me and catches me staring. I pretend that I was looking past her. She goes back to her conversation and I look at my boots. Patricia's right, they do need to be cleaned. I just want to go home. I just want to go home. I tap my heels three times. And then, like a Bribie Island bream, they reel me back in.

Rachel, Matt's offering to give you free piano lessons, says Angus eagerly.

I look up.

Matt's been playing the piano since he was five. Haven't you, Matt? says Claire.

I look at Matt. He smiles and shrugs. I decide that he looks a little like Hugh Jackman. But less cute.

It's a tricky piece. I just thought that you could use a little help, he says. *Since you're trying to win a bet.*

'So what you're saying is that you think I need help. You think I'm crap at piano?'

No, it's just that I've been listening to you practise and it's a tricky piece and I could hear that even the first bar was giving you trouble; but no, I don't think you're crap at piano. I think you have crap taste in music …

His face is deadpan. And then his lips betray him as they curve into a half smile.

... but apart from that, I was just thinking that I could help you out and, you know, lessons would be a good distraction for me.

'From what?'

He opens his mouth to say something and then shuts it again, as if to think better of it. And then he says, *A distraction from my studies. And Bert Newton. I sit at home writing my thesis paper and I find the words Big Kev's Goo Remover creeping into paragraphs about the structural advantages of eighteenth-century bridges. And I've started looking forward to Belvedere's poems and it's a worrying thing. You'd be doing me a favour.*

Maybe.

'What's the catch?' I say.

No catch, he says smiling, his two hands up in front of his chest as if he's pleading his innocence or saying 'look Mum, no hands'.

I'm skeptical. And I tell my face to act accordingly.

Why would there have to be a catch?

Hmmm.

'I'll think about it', I say. I suspect that the price is too high. I'm not sure I want Mr Chipped-tooth-Hugh Jackman-lookalike-piano-player in my life. In my house. Judging me and my Bedazzler. I look over at him and he is looking at me. His face resting on his hands. I can tell from his eyes that he's analyzing me, he's not looking at me, he's trying to look into me. He's trying to work me out. I think he thinks I'm a big dickhead. Sure. I am a big dickhead. I should go.

Okay, well I should go. The offer is there, Rachel. My computer crashed this afternoon, so if you want lessons, give me a call. He grabs a pen from his back pocket and scribbles his phone number onto the back of an RE coaster. *If we do the lessons together that would be great and if not, then it was nice meeting you and I'm sure I'll be hearing strains of Rick Astley coming from your house sometime real soon.* And then Matt gets up.

It was nice to meet you. He smiles at Angus and Claire. *And Rachel, I'll see you 'round. Maybe.* As he walks past me he pulls my baseball cap down over my eyes. Something I always do to Alex.

He saunters off through the crowd.

'Aren't you even going to tell me which house you live in?' I ask his back.

Nope. And he laughs and keeps walking.

14

Naturally, all day Sunday, the idea of ringing Matt and asking for help is on my mind. I stare at the digits he's written on the back of the RE coaster and wonder how it is that some kids grow up crossing their number sevens, like a misplaced 't', and others don't.

I practise 'Jessica's Theme' for a long time on Sunday. Zoë rings and bugs me again about reading her latest literary offering to the world of erotic fiction. I tell her I'm too busy today. She threatens to come over and read it to me aloud. If there is one thing worse than reading Zoë's porn, it's hearing Zoë read it out loud. With the different voices.

'Aren't you supposed to be booking someone's airfare?'

Shit. And with that she hangs up on me, as if it just occurred to her that the money that gets deposited into her bank account every second Thursday wasn't just good luck. Somebody was paying her to do something other than pen porn.

And so I go back to feeling like a failure. I have three weeks to master this piece perfectly and commit it to memory and I'm not getting it. As much as the thought of Matt snooping around in my life grates on me, right now my need to achieve this goal is winning out.

Do I ring? Do I ring? Do I ring?

I'm tempted to toss a coin. Tempted to find a sign in the most mundane. I'll take the lessons if the phone rings again before two pm. If a certain song comes on the radio. If I get a Pizza Hut coupon in my letterbox today in between the usual Retravision and A-Mart Allsports flyers. If I could bloody well just get through the first page of 'Jessica's Theme' without stuffing up.

It's hard to believe that I was ever a great decision-maker but I was. I had a reputation for being able to make snap decisions; I had to as the Features Editor. There was no room for dilly-dallying. No room for 'umm, I just don't know'. I was paid to know. And I trusted my judgment. I pulled stories. I changed photo spreads. I've stopped a print-run to change an advertisement. I was in that job because of my decision-making ability. That same decision-making ability which got me into so much trouble in Las Vegas.

Things are different now. Now I tend to trust the judgment of everyone else. Anyone who isn't me.

I go to the fridge and take out the yellow envelope. I read through the papers from Moss & French solicitors firm in

Los Angeles. Joel Moss and Pat French who I will never meet, never talk to on the phone but who are currently arranging my divorce from Mr Troy Shepherd. There are at least a dozen forms here. On some of them I am referred to as the respondent. On others I am referred to as 'wife'. I see the name of the church and the date. For a few seconds I close my eyes and picture the day. What I was wearing. Troy's smile. The minister. The feeling of nausea I had when the whole thing was over and done with.

The cold air seeps out from the fridge and envelopes me in a chilly embrace. I open my eyes and look back down at the papers. I look at the Miss Brisbane Awards fundraising timetable that I have stuck up on the fridge door. I look into the lounge room at the digital piano.

My life is a mess. I have to regain control and this piece is the first step. I'm going to make the call.

And it's a disaster.

For one thing, I get tongue-tied when Matt answers the phone and end up telling him I want to discuss the liano pessons. But worse than that, Matt tells me that he's changed his mind.

Now there's a condition.

15

He gets to ask me how many people I've slept with.

Let me rephrase that.

OHMYGOD. He gets to ask me how many people I've slept with.

You're very difficult to get to know. I think you're a little too uptight, he said. *Stand-offish, tense*, he said.

'Bite me,' I said.

And those two words sealed my fate. Matt decides that in return for free lessons, he should be allowed to ask me a question. Since that's the only way he's going to be able to find out anything about me, neighbour to neighbour. Since I'm not exactly brimming with friendliness. One question, before every lesson. One question, before every lesson, that

I have to answer. And then he said he'd see me at ten am and hung up. And he doesn't actually specify the question. But I know the type of thing it will be. He's gonna ask me how many people I've slept with. Or when I lost my virginity. Or if I was ever tempted to get married in Vegas in front of Elvis.

I feel sick. It's probably scurvy. God's doing payback. I can't remember when the last time was that I ate an orange. Do I have a fever? I think I have a fever.

Rachel! Ask me!

Oranges can't be the only things that have Vitamin C. I think I'm dying. What the fuck have I been doing all these years eating bananas and apples? Oh God. I can't breathe.

RACHEL!

The sound of Alex's voice brings me back to the job at hand. It's Monday morning at the Moore household and I'm supposed to be testing Alex on her spelling. We're sitting at the breakfast table which is a jumble of Vegemite jars and margarine tubs with suspicious black splodges and toast crumbs and sticky spots of honey and jam and a grubby-looking coffee cup with a few inches of dark brown mud in the bottom, all competing for space. Dressed in her green checked school uniform, Alex sits happily amongst it all, perched on her knees on the chair, jam-stained fingers gripped around a purple crayon, drawing ants. Great purple ants. Ants that have hair and wear hats and lipstick. She puts her crayon down dramatically and looks up at me.

Rachel!

'Okay, keep your pants on.' I pick up her spelling book

and resume the alphabet inquisition. 'How do you spell "scurvy"?'

What?

'Nothing. Just something I'm dying from. Forget it. How do you spell "tall"?'

T-A-L — she pauses for a moment, possibly for effect — *L.*

'Excellent job. You are one smart cookie, Alex.'

A gap-toothed smile spreads across her entire face for a few seconds, before she resumes her serious artist-renowned-for-ant-sketches expression.

'Now, how do you spell "fall"?'

Alex takes a big gulp of Milo, looks up at me and says *F-A-L-L,* burping the letters with terrifying, yet frankly not unimpressive, accuracy.

'Alex,' I say, rolling my eyes and sighing. 'Now spell the next one properly. How about "ball"?'

She puts down her crayon. *Snowy and I want some Coke.*

Here we go.

'No. No Coke for breakfast. You can have some when you get home for afternoon tea. Now how do you spell "ball"?'

B-A-L-L, says Alex, getting up from her chair and walking calmly over to the fridge.

'Alex, I said N-O C-O-K-E.'

She looks at me with defiant eyes, as she opens the fridge door, reaching for the three-litre Coke bottle.

'Don't do it, Alex. I'm warning you.'

With two arms she carries the bottle over to the kitchen bench, waddling like a pregnant woman carrying triplets.

She bangs the bottle down on the laminate surface with a Monica-Seles-style groan, before plucking her Disney glass from a cupboard underneath.

'If you pour yourself a glass of Coke, I'll tell your mum.'

Her lips tighten, her forehead wrinkles and even her freckles look pissed off. She unscrews the cap and with both hands on the bottle, lifts it up shakily to pour herself a glass, spilling Coke all over the bench top. She looks at me defiantly, her eyes shining, before lifting the glass up to her lips.

'Drink that Coke and there'll be no *Funniest Home Video Show*.'

She freezes. I've found her Achilles heel. I can see her little six-year-old mind ticking over. What's worth more? Sugary forbidden drink or an hour of watching babies fall off swings and brides tripping over and flashing their knickers. It's no contest.

You're not the boss of me. She looks at me, her face beginning to crumple and quiver with anger and her freckles transform into teardrops and slowly plop off her face. *It's unfair. You're dumb. I hate you.* She slams the glass back on the table and turns her back on the Coke bottle in Sophia-Loren-angry-jilted-Italian-vixen-fashion and strides past me before slamming her bedroom door. Snowy trots after her but not before giving me a backwards cursory glance that says it all. *Coke rules. Bitch.*

In the car on the way to school Alex refuses to talk to me until I let her put on some of my strawberry lip-gloss. And then allow her to take it to school so that Emma can try it. And then tell her that she can keep it.

As we drive, I try and impress Alex by telling her about some of the celebrities that I've interviewed in the past for the magazine. Kylie Minogue, Ian Thorpe, Sigrid Thornton, Rove McManus.

Have you interviewed Cleopatra? She turns and looks at me hopefully, eyebrows raised.

'No,' I say a little off-handedly, contemplating the Kenmore Village roundabout. 'She's dead.'

Alex stares at me as if I killed Cleopatra myself. As if I grabbed that hungry asp and whispered to it, 'Nummy-nummy, Cleopatra,' before throwing it at the Egyptian Queen's throat. She turns back to look out the window and reapplies her lip-gloss like a bored supermodel.

She's warming to me, I can feel it.

It's not until I get home at about 9.15am that I start panicking again about Matt. And the first question.

16

Matt knocks at the door at exactly ten am. And when I look through the peephole all I can see is orange. When I open the door I am faced with Matt juggling oranges and lemons while he sings that stupid song with lyrics about drunken sailors and hooray-up-she-rises.

'What are you doing?'

It's a peace offering. He smiles. And winks. I hate winkers. They're one small vowel away from being something far nastier.

It was a toss up between these and a Choose Life T-shirt. But more important to keep your scurvy at bay, I think. He hands me the fruit and strolls into the hallway. *And did you notice that this time I stuck to the path?*

While I'm left staring at the citrus offering, Matt has walked past me and into the house. He calls out to me from the kitchen.

Did you make these? Matthew Harding is now sitting on the kitchen bench eating some of Patricia's almond bread.

'No I didn't. Are you ...' I pause, trying to think of something other than A.D.D.

Very 60s split level, he says, looking around him. *This is a really great house. Are you going to show me around?*

Matt has been in my house for less than a minute and already I'm tensing up. 'Let's go back into the music room.'

Matt looks like he's going to say something but instead just scratches his unshaven chin and nods. *Okay, enough mucking around. Where's the liano?*

I ignore this and start stressing about the condition. The question. I want to stall. But he's already sitting down at the piano, looking over the music. Maybe he's forgotten? I sit on the edge of a lounge chair. My mouth feels dry and my heart is racing. If he asks me anything too personal, I'm just going to tell him to leave.

So, he says, rubbing his hands together dramatically. *I get to ask you a question, which you have to answer. Ready?*

'Just ask it. But I'm not answering anything too personal. And nothing rude.'

What was Skippy's surname on Family Ties*?*

'WHAT?'

Skippy's surname on Family Ties*. What was it? You remember Skippy, the neighbour who was in love with Mallory.*

'That's it? That's the question? You could ask me anything at all and you're asking me about an 80s sitcom?'

Sure. And stop stalling.

'It was, um, Handelman. Skippy Handelman.'

Very good. What's the first line of the theme song?

'Well I bet we've been together for a million years,' rolls off my tongue far too easily. 'How is it that I can remember the entire theme song to *Family Ties* but I can't recall what a prime number is?'

Matt looks edgy. He bites his lower lip.

'Don't tell me. I don't want to know. Ask me another question.'

What did Angela do for a living on Who's the Boss? he demands before adding, *Numbers which can only be divided by themselves and one.*

'She worked in advertising. You're wasting my time. For double points, on the same show, what was the name of Angela's mother?'

Three.

'What?'

Three, five, seven, eleven. That's a few examples. Of prime numbers. Numbers that can only be divided by themselves or one.

'Thank you Rainman, now answer the question.'

Forty-five.

'Forty-five is not a prime number.'

Yeah I know, that's the number of the house I live in.

'Oh.'

Back to the question. Her name was Mona. I spent my entire childhood in front of the TV. They didn't call me Maggie Magnetised for nothing.

We both pause. He looks at me like someone who has just accidentally confessed to wetting the bed as a child.

As in magnetised to the television. I used to sit so close to the screen that my mother said I was magnetised to it. Enough about me, look at you. You've gone from nervous to smug. You're forcing me to bring out the big guns, you know.

'Try me.'

I'm moving to something way more difficult.

'Fine.'

What city was Mork and Mindy *set in?*

Bastard, I think to myself. I visualise the opening credits, the jeep, the egg landing in the field, Mork sitting in the car on his head and the sign. The sign that said … Welcome to …

'Boulder, Colorado, thank you very much. You totally picked the wrong show. I was a dedicated Mork from Ork fan.'

Me too. I had the rainbow braces and the whole nanoo-nanoo handshake thing going. Which is okay when you're ten but not so cool when it's your school formal.

'You're not serious?'

No. He laughs and then looks back at me slyly. *Maybe.*

We both smile at each other.

'Yeah, you know a few months ago I won the major prize at a trivia night because — this is really funny — I was the only person in the room who could sing the *Mork and Mindy* theme song! They were giving away $100 to the first person who could sing it and I was the only person who put their hand up. It was pretty funny. Where were you that night, huh?'

He nods and then swings back around to face the keys. *So, where are you having the most trouble?* He flicks through the sheet music of 'Jessica's Theme': Breaking in the Colt. Hair falls in front of his eyes. He pushes it back off his face.

'You don't remember it, do you?'

Sure I remember it. He scratches his arm. I'm pretty sure it is the scratch of someone who couldn't distinguish Arnold Drummond from Webster.

'Good one. Good one, Maggie. You don't know it.' And I start laughing out loud. A boisterous laugh that Patricia would hate. The laugh of someone who doesn't get out much.

I DO know it.

'Then sing it.'

Okay. He pauses. Closes his eyes and starts humming and then singing vague words about Mork from Ork. Words that have nothing to do with the theme song. Or any song. Ever. In the history of songs. When he starts on a chorus which has the words fork, pork and cork, I decide enough is enough.

'You're crap,' I say. 'You're making that song up. There is no sitcom theme song that has ever had the word "pork" in it.'

He looks at me guiltily.

Just start me off and I'll get it. Just give me the opening bars.

'Nope. Not happening. I can't believe you don't know it.

That's pathetic. You're such an amateur. I win.' And I feel a surge of superiority. A level of superiority I haven't felt since I caught Zoë singing the wrong words to a Cold Chisel song. Zoë spent a decade thinking that 'Cheap wine and a three day growth' was actually 'Cheap wine and a three-day roast'. Which is fine to sing in the privacy of your own car but asking for trouble if you sing it at a Chisel concert.

And now I'm ready to start the lesson.

The lesson is far from smooth. Matt wants me to play the piece all the way through and I refuse. I want to tackle it section by section. He wants to discuss the piece as a whole, talk about the feel of it, the mood that it's trying to convey.

Whatever.

I'm not playing the piece all the way through for him. I stink. Nobody gets to hear the entire thing. Not until I can play it perfectly.

We argue for an hour about my fractured approach, while I play the first page over and over. The end result is that I can now play the first six bars with barely any mistakes. And I have acquired the new skill of arguing and playing piano simultaneously.

When my fingers are tired, Matt takes the seat. And without saying a word, he just starts playing. As if to show me how he thinks Jessica would want her theme to sound. Or maybe he just wants to impress me, I can't tell. But he sits there and his awkward, over-sized hands — classic gardener's hands, a bit like Patricia's with bites and cuts and scratches — start to move. His fingers skip along the keys, dancing like children let loose in a playground, like his fingertips are being reunited with their best neighbourhood pals. And his music fills the room up as if it's water being poured into a long tall glass. It seeps into every corner, every gap and crevice in the room, in a way that Morton Harket or Huey Lewis never could.

I close my eyes and listen. Swept away, a weak swimmer paddling against a bossy current. The music pushes me along and out to sea, the quavers and crochets whirling around my ears like seagulls. I feel like I am drowning and flying all at once. Drowning and flying.

Rachel.

Rachel.

Someone touches my arm. I come back and realise the music has stopped. And I still have my eyes closed. Damn. This is so embarrassing. I open one eye and look at him. What am I, a pirate? I open the other eye. I now have both eyes open, just like a normal, sane person. A person who wouldn't even consider getting married using the pull-ring of a Coke can.

You must really love this piece. You were smiling. As you were listening to it. Matt is leaning into me. His eyes are focused on me intently, urging me to open up, make a confession, connect with him just for a moment on a deeper level.

'Is that the time?' I get up from the couch, and walk over to the front door. 'Thanks for coming.'

Okay, he says, realising that he's being booted out. *Uh, Rachel? Can I give you a piece of advice?*

'What's that?'

Good piano playing isn't just about hitting the right notes —

it's about letting the piece's real personality come through. I just want you to know that.

'Sure Matt,' I say. 'I'll see you tomorrow.'

17

I spend a quiet night at home on Monday night. I order a pizza and debate whether or not to go the anchovies. I watch *Friends* repeats and laugh to myself at Monica's hair and Phoebe's clothes. The phone rings. No sooner do I put the receiver to my ear than a familiar voice says *I've got it!* followed by some robust, but still fairly awful, humming. And then I am treated to …

Show me that smile again, don't waste another minute on your crying, we're nowhere near the …

'Matt, that would be the *Growing Pains* theme song you're singing. Not *Mork and Mindy*.'

Shit, he says a little too seriously. *Okay, okay how about, Now the world don't move to the beat of just one drum, what might be right for you, may not be right for some, a …*

'You know perfectly well that's *Different Strokes*.'

Whatchoo talkin' about Willis?

'I'm hanging up now, Matt.'

Just give me the first word. Or the first three words. Three words Rachel. Come on!

And I can't help but smile as I hang up the phone.

18

At 6.15am on Tuesday, Sharon rings to tell me that I am not needed today or tomorrow because she has a cold and she's taking two days off. But on Thursday she has to work back. So could I pick Alex up from school and then look after her until about five? No worries.

I decide to spend the morning doing useful things. Being productive. I type up my Miss Brisbane Awards fundraising ideas and media tips for the other entrants and email them to Jan. And then I take out my knitting. Knitting, I think, is a totally misunderstood activity. It gets no respect. It needs a good PR agent. I could do PR for knitting, I think. And I would use Julia Roberts as my spokesperson. I read an article on her in *In Style* magazine that says she is a knitter from way back. So Julia Roberts, when she's not on safari in Mongolia or hanging out with orang-utans, could be the face of knitting in the 21st century.

At nine am my old boss calls from *Escape* magazine. Karen. She wants to know if I will do next month's celebrity interview.

So we were thinking about a sportsperson. Susie O'Neill, Grant Hackett – someone like that. Whaddyathink?

'Well, yeah, I suppose they'd be good but they're really difficult to get. Because they're not promoting anything. They don't have a reason to do the interview. That's why TV people, film people, authors, they're easier to get. They're trying to flog something.'

What about Georgie Parker?

'Yeah she'd be good ... hey, you know who's doing the rounds at the moment? Dave Howard. The author. He'd be great.'

Never heard of him.

'Well, no, he's not huge. Yet. But he's up and coming. He's a local Brisbane author. His first book sold heaps of copies. It's become a bit of a cult thing.'

Okay, well, let me know who his publisher is and I'll see if I can set it up for you. Stay tuned.

Ten minutes after I hang up from Karen, Jan calls.

Rachel Hill, how are you? She says my name far too enthusiastically, as if on my birth certificate there are exclamation marks after my Christian name and my surname. Unwarranted enthusiasm aside, she wants to thank me for sending through the email with the tips for the other entrants. And then she adds, *Tempted to organise a garage sale or quiz night yourself?*

'Oh, well, I've organised to do some fundraising but I'm just finalising the details at the moment,' I say, amazing myself at how easily that big fat fib rolls off my tongue.

Okay, says Jan. *Well remember that we need you to raise a minimum of $500 if you even want a chance at qualifying as the Corinda District entrant. For some districts, where there are a lot of girls competing, the girl who raises the most money gets to go through to the next round.*

'Really?' I say. 'So, what you're saying is that if I don't raise $500 then I automatically don't get to go through? To the next round?'

Exactly! says Jan. *You have to raise at least $500. Now, do you have the fundraising timetable?*

'Yep,' I say, scrunching it up in my hand and throwing it into the bin.

Okay. Well, call us if you need any help. We're here to help you. We're just a phone call away.

'Fabulous,' I reply. And then I tell her that I must go and wax my upper lip.

19

Tuesday's lesson with Matthew is much better. He arrives late looking tired.

Uni-student-cramming-for-exams-all-night-and-taken-too-much-NoDoze kinda tired.

'You look exhausted,' I say, as he steps past me and into the kitchen. I notice that he has a cut on the side of his face, near his eye.

In Different Strokes *what was the name of Arnold's goldfish?* he calls back over his shoulder as he heads for the almond bread.

'Abraham. Can we get started now? Or did you want to sing me the *Mork and Mindy* theme song? Oh, that's right,' I say slapping my head in mock frustration, 'You don't know it.'

He turns around but not before he catches sight of my knitting, which is minding its own business, sitting on the kitchen bench near the phone. He looks at the knitting. He looks at me. He says, *You're very smug for someone who knits.*

I protectively snatch up my scarf work-in-progress and clutch it to my bosom. I tell him that Julia Roberts knits. That she is a knitter from way back. That she is one of the most beautiful women in the world and earns $40m a picture but that maybe she'd be earning $45m a picture if everyone knew that she could whip up a jumper, vest and matching scarf in record time.

What is it? he says, trying to grab it from me like an annoying younger brother.

'It's a scarf. For Caitlin. My sister. And you don't get to look at it since you're making fun of it. And you're supposed to be amazed at the fact that I knew the name of the Drummond boys' goldfish.'

Good point. I can't believe you knew that. Did you actually leave the house as a child? He moves past me and back into the lounge room and over to the piano.

'You're just pissed off because you can't remember the Mork theme.'

He turns and does an 'is that right?' type of face.

Let's make a bet. You think you're so smart. If you don't get every question correct over the five lessons, you have to play me the piece all the way through.

'Fine,' I say.

We shake hands and I secretly pray that Matthew Harding wasn't a big fan of *Charles in Charge*.

Today's lesson lasts three hours. Mainly because Matt refuses to go home.

'Go home,' I say repeatedly.

No, he says.

'Don't you have a thesis to write?'

Don't you have a piano piece to learn?

'Fine. Stay then.' And a tiny part of me is as pleased as a six-year-old with new lip-gloss.

And, as we sit at the piano and I practise the first page over and over and over and Matt corrects my finger-work and mutters *slow it down* under his breath, we talk. Or rather, Matt talks and I listen. I'm not quite sure if I am the one feeding him questions, like a mother spooning baby glup into a three-month-old's mouth, but somehow words and not notes start to spill from Matthew Harding. And when I repeatedly stumble over some difficult chords (which I feel are ganging up on me when Matthew's back is turned), he says, *Move over* and sits next to me on the bench and takes my hand and places it on his forearm and makes me play the chords on his skin. He doesn't tell me why we are doing this. Or perhaps he does but I'm not listening. Instead, as my fingers tap into his arm, I breathe in his aftershave and wonder how it is that this man came to be sitting in my house. A man who isn't Troy.

I learn a lot about this not-Troy today. In a patchwork-quilt kind of way. He reveals cuttings from his life – little snippets that sewn together form something bigger. I hear that he is twenty-six years old, that he is studying engineering but did two years at the Conservatorium of Music before changing course. Why? I want to ask. Did you want to be a pianist? What made you change your mind? But I don't ask and instead I listen and stare at the sheets in front of me and keep practising. I hear that he is an only child. That when he was five his best friend Mark tricked him into eating a dog biscuit. I hear that he has his father's Irish temper; that almond bread reminds him of his grandmother who died a few years back; that, as a child, when he wasn't watching television, he was a big Archie comics fan; and that he thinks fruit, pineapple or otherwise, has no place in the world of pizza toppings.

So tell me about you, he says. As if he really thinks it's going to be that easy. As if me using his arm for keyboard practise minutes earlier is a natural segue into sharing.

I stop playing just for a moment and contemplate my options. Tell me about you. What part of me am I meant to share? What is it that he wants to know? At this precise moment, who is he hoping that I will be? Because in those minutes, hours, days when we first meet someone new, we ache with the possibility of who they might be and whether the person that they present to us will be the right answer. Even when we never tell them the question to start off with. I'm not his new person. He should know that. In case he thinks he's putting in all this legwork so that he'll get laid at the end of it or something. So I say the only thing I can say.

'I'm great at tunnel ball.'

That's the only patch he's getting.

He smiles, as if I have made a mildly amusing joke that

he doesn't really think is funny. Or maybe he just hates tunnel ball. It's too soon to tell.

We sit. The air is heavy with his disappointment that I have not shared more. And I actually feel bad about that. Perhaps someone else can come in and give him the low-down on me. Like Zoë. Or Mike Munro. Mike could walk in with the big red book and proclaim *Rachel Hill, THIS is your life*. And I could be the first person to say 'Fuck off, Mike'. This thought cheers me up. Until I realise that Mike's not here. And anyway, I don't have any stories about Caitlin feeding me dog biscuits. Although, when I was seven and she was five, I did dare her to eat an entire block of cheddar cheese, which she subsequently spewed up all over the kitchen lino. But I don't feel like sharing. Not today. Not with Matt. I don't understand what's going on here.

Seconds tiptoe past us. Fill the page Rachel. Nobody likes to look at a blank page. Do your job.

'Betty or Veronica?'

What?

'Betty or Veronica? If you were Archie and you had to choose between Betty and Veronica, who would you choose?' I ask this question, my voice weighed down with suspicion, as if the answer is unofficially part of a Myers-Briggs test and will reveal a lot about Matthew Harding's psyche.

Oh that's easy. He looks up at me with a smile in his eyes only to be greeted with my 'I'm gonna hook you up to a polygraph machine' intensity. *Oh, fuck, right, well, hang on, let me have another think about it,* says Matt, disturbed by the look in my eye. Minutes pass.

Okay, here's my answer. I wouldn't choose Betty — she was cute but a little needy. And I wouldn't choose Veronica — she was cool but a complete bitch. So I'd have to say that I'd look past the orthodontic problems and I'd choose Big Ethel. I love a girl who loves her food. Headgear or no headgear.

'Big Ethel didn't wear headgear.'

Yeah? Well she should have.

'Good point.'

Now, what's for lunch?

20

Two ham and cheese sandwiches, a banana smoothie and a debate about the superiority of Coke over Pepsi later and Matt's gone. I find myself looking forward to tomorrow's lesson. I look in the mirror. I look a bit scruffy. When did I stop caring about my appearance? My thick brown hair is tied in a careless lumpy knot out of my face – except for a few scraggly bits. So I push them back behind my ears, smooth down my shirt. I start thinking about what I should wear tomorrow. Maybe my pink Esprit shirt and white shorts. Maybe my Women In Docs T-shirt and jeans. Maybe a white dress with a matching veil. That's me. Always on the lookout for a second husband.

I call Karen to find out the latest on the Dave Howard interview.

The publicist said that if you email him the questions tomorrow he'd do them for you within 24 hours. She said that you can ask him about his next book Perfect Summer *and as many travel questions as you want. She said he's done a lot of travel. He's been to India, I think. And I gave them your mobile number just in case of anything. In case there's any problems. And his publicist said that I could give you his mobile, in case you want to ring him. In case you need to clarify anything over the phone.*

Karen reads out Dave Howard's email address and phone number and I jot them down.

So have you thought of any other ideas for stories? she says.

'Sure. I was thinking of something global.'

Global's good.

'Sure, global's great. So I was thinking maybe something about food around the world. I was eating some Miracle Whip the other night and I ...'

Miracle what?

'Miracle Whip. It's like mayonnaise.

Right ...

'Anyway, I was looking at the jar and I thought to myself, I bet you have a website and I got on-line and there was. There was a Miracle Whip website. With a world map with flashing red dots in the countries where Miracle Whip can be purchased.'

There is silence on the other end.

'It's a great website, Karen. It has the history of Miracle Whip and recipe ideas. Like a chocolate cake with Miracle

Whip in it. And there's a map. Did I mention the map already? Like in Panama, they have a special pouch called the *facilitas* that they put their Miracle Whip in.'

Rachel. You're telling me you want to do a story on Great Mayonnaises of the World?

This is Karen's problem. She doesn't listen properly.

'Karen, don't be ridiculous. Nobody is going to be interested in reading a "Great Mayonnaises of the World" article.'

Exactly.

'No, I'm talking about honing in on Miracle Whip. See, I was thinking that we could start looking at popular food items that are, well, popular. And we could do stories about them. You know, like where they come from. So we could start with Miracle Whip. And then we could do Vegemite. But we should start with Miracle Whip and we should talk about how it was invented and where you can find it. Like if you're in Mexico and you're having a tortilla and you just want something on that tortilla to sweeten it up. You can get your Spanish version of Miracle Whip.'

From the local 7-11.

'Well no, I'm pretty sure that they're not called 7-11. What's seven in Spanish?'

I'm sure I don't know.

'I should be able to remember. The Spanish guy on *Sesame Street* was counting in Spanish the other morning. What's his name? Manuel. Yeah. No, it's not. It's Luis. Oh my God, he is sex on a stick. Have you seen him? I know I haven't had sex in over six months but I could seriously do Luis. It's the accent …'

I hear a laugh in the background and someone mutters *Christ, she's become so pathetic* … It sounds like Simon from Accounts.

'Karen?'

Yes, Rachel?

'Have you put me on speaker-phone?'

I can hear a few gasps and some stifled giggles.

Rachel, we're all worried about you.

She pauses.

Rachel, you're talking about having sex with a Sesame Street character.

'Luis isn't a character. He's a real person. It's not like I said I wanted to root Grover, Karen. Luis is a real person, with real feelings and real needs. Just like all of us. He's just a man, Karen. Just a man.'

This is a difficult time for you. I know that. I heard about Troy. That you broke up.

'Well, we didn't. We're still together. He loves me a lot. He wants to marry me.'

I hang up the phone. I sit on the floor by my bed. Why would I say that?

I wish Troy or Zoë or Angus or Claire or Mum or Dad or Caitlin was here.

Or even Matt. I'd settle for Matt.

21

On Wednesday, her RDO, I invite Zoë over to play.

Where's Matt?

'He left about 10 minutes ago.'

How'd it go?

'Yeah. Okay.' I think about today's question. He was so sure I wouldn't get it. Naming three Wombles was tough but I got there eventually. Orinoco and Great Uncle Bulgaria are the easy ones. Not many people can remember Wellington or Bungo. He was horrified. It was a good lesson, though. He always makes me laugh.

Look at your face. You're having sex with him, aren't you?

'What? No! No. Jesus, Zee. No. It's piano lessons. That's all.'

Sure. I know all about "piano lessons", she says doing inverted commas with her fingers. *Hey, I've seen* The Piano. *I know what goes on.*

' "Scales," ' I say, doing the inverted commas back to her. 'That's what goes on. Scales and boring repetitive practise. Just give me your story to read.'

It's here. On disk. Read it now. While I'm here.

'Why is it on disk? Don't you have a hard copy?'

Shaun says that I'm not allowed to print out my erotic fiction on the work printer. You know, because of what happened last time. When Lisa accidentally stapled page two of one of my stories with a customer's Contiki Tour itinerary.

'Bugger.'

One minute this guy was reading about the two-night stay at a youth hostel in Salzburg, Austria, and the next minute he was reading about Philomena.

'… the human zucchini cannon?'

Yeah. Lisa was pretty upset. Especially since the next week the customer left a zucchini on her desk with his phone number written in pen on the side.

'Just so you know. Since I read that story, I haven't been able to eat zucchini.'

Really? Thanks. She grins. Somehow, Zoë takes this as a compliment. The fact that her story was so stomach-churning that it put me off an entire variety of vegetable is a good thing in her mind. I've quickly learnt that in Zee's world there is no line of distinction between sexual aids and fruit'n'veg. Needless to say, she is banned from bringing coleslaw to BBQs.

'I can't read it now, I've just sent an email to Dave Howard introducing myself and I told him that I would be sending through the interview questions this afternoon. So my mind's on that. Did I tell you that I was doing an email interview with him for the magazine? Karen arranged it. Anyway, leave the disk with me and I'll read it later.'

Do you think he'll remember you? Are you going to tell him that he signed your book last week? That you were the mute weird girl who likened herself to the Pied Piper?

'No, of course not. I'm going to play it cool. Professional. I've interviewed heaps of celebrities before. This is not a big deal. And it's only over email. So … hand over the disk.'

I can't. I've gotta send the disk in with the entry form. I'll download a copy on your computer. How's that? I'll do it now.

'Fine.'

She goes downstairs to the computer, while I make us a sandwich. As I cut up some tomato, I hear Zoë laughing to herself.

She comes back upstairs. *Promise me you'll read it. It'll make you laugh. So,* she says, leaning on the kitchen bench, *did you get out of the Miss Brisbane thing?*

'Not yet.'

But you are going to quit, right? You know that you're not eligible to be in the award? Right?

'I know. But I'm just helping some of the other entrants. With their fundraising and media stuff. Cause, you know, that's my area of expertise.'

Zoë looks doubtful.

'Do you want mustard pickle on your sandwich?'

Yep. You know, I think I'd make a good Miss Brisbane. She hoists herself up on the kitchen bench to watch me while I cut our sandwiches in half before handing her one.

'Yeah right. Yeah, you'd be good. You've got all the decorum they're looking for.'

I've got a shitload more decorum than you.

'You've got pickle on your chin.'

Oh fuck. She tries to reach it with her tongue before wiping it with the back of her hand.

Name one time when I haven't acted with 100% sophistication.

'The day you mooned the crowd of people queuing for Michael Bolton tickets outside Myer. The time you got drunk at the Casino, pulled down your knickers and tried to do a wee in the same potplant your favourite football player had urinated in the week before. The time you got us kicked out of that cinema …'

When?

'When? When we went to see *The Doors* and you started pegging malteasers at the screen, yelling out, 'Hurry up and get in the fucking bath you bastard' whenever Jim Morrison was on screen.'

Yeah, but it was a long movie. I was bored.

I look at her dubiously.

Fair enough. She sighs and looks a little downcast. But then she lifts her head up and smiles and says, *But I give good zucchini.*

'And the Brisbane Fruit and Vegetable Association thanks you for that. You are the Poster Girl for People Who Do Rude Things With Oblong Vegetables.'

We sit in the kitchen in silence for a few minutes eating our lunch.

I wish I had your job. I'm much better at mingling with celebrities than you. You never know what to say. Look how great I was with Kylie.

'Loitering outside the security gates at the Brisbane Entertainment Centre and yelling out *Show us your pink bits* to Kylie Minogue – I'm pretty sure that's not mingling.'

She smiled at me, though.

'No, she smiled at the security guard who told you to watch your mouth.'

Still …

'Still, in your world, that counts for something. And a restraining order, that's just someone playing hard to get.'

When Zoë leaves, I head back down to the computer to check if Dave Howard has emailed me back and to send him the interview questions.

When I get on-line there is one email. It's from Dave Howard.

Subject: Re: interview
Date: Wednesday 12.18pm
From: DaveHoward@yoohoo.net
To: RachelHill@mymail.com.au

Hi Rachel
Thanks for your email. I'm around most of this afternoon, so just send through the questions anytime. It's probably best if you send them as a Word attachment. Your name seems

familiar to me. Have we met before or do I just recognise your name from your articles in *Escape*?
Dave

Oh shit.

What do I do? Do I fess up to the book signing or do I deny all knowledge of the encounter? What if I say we haven't met before and then he remembers? Remembers me. The weird Pied Piper girl.

I'm screwed. I go on-line.

Subject: Re re: interview
Date: Wednesday 12.48pm
From: RachelHill@mymail.com.au
To: DaveHoward@yoohoo.net

Hi Dave
You caught me! I'm actually a bit of a fan. You signed a book of mine at Indooroopilly last week. Does Rachel Hill – Pied Piper girl sound familiar? I could have kicked myself for being so nervous!
Rachel

I press send. I realise that I forgot to send the interview questions. I decide to wait and see what his response will be to my confession. Thirty minutes pass. Nothing. I check my email like a nervous new mother checking that her baby is breathing. I watch television. I pace around the kitchen. I practise piano. I wash up. Still nothing. I look at Dave Howard's phone number. It would be terrible if I lost this. I should really key it into my mobile. In case he rings. He might ring. And then I'll know it's him. His name will come up. Then I can make sure that I sound professional when I answer it. I add Dave Howard's name to my mobile phone speed dial. I log on again. Still no response. Damn.

I decide to go for a walk. As I'm walking down the driveway, I see a young blonde woman coming out of Matt's house. She's beautiful. Naturally, I hate her. I watch her walk down their front path – then I hear Matt call out. At first I think he is calling out to me. But then I see that he is calling to Blondie. I hide behind the wheelie bins and watch. He appears at the screen door and calls her back. I hear him say something about being really sorry. Her eyes look red and puffy. She touches his arm and says something to him. I can't hear what she's saying. And then she turns around and walks to her car. A red Laser. He goes back inside.

I didn't know he had a girlfriend. Or maybe it's a sister. Can't be, he's an only child. So, Matt has a girlfriend. I wonder why he never told me. And I wonder what he's sorry about. Maybe he burnt her toast this morning. Maybe he forgot to put out the rubbish or forgot her birthday. Maybe he's sorry that he made her orgasm three times in a row when they had sex on the kitchen bench thirty minutes ago. I walk back into the house feeling … what? Sad? Lonely? No, disappointed. I feel disappointed. I look up Dave Howard's name on my mobile. It cheers me up. Hitting the green 'call' key is all that separates Dave Howard and me. Yep.

I go back to the computer and get online. It's now an hour and a half since I sent Dave Howard my last email. My confession about the Pied Piper incident. There is something in my In Box. I have two messages. The first one is from Ally, some joke about owners who look like their dogs. The second email is from somebody called Jemima Taylor.

> Subject:
> Date: Wednesday 1.31pm
> From: Jemima Taylor taylor@prnet.net
> To: RachelHill@ mymail.com.au
>
> Hello Rachel
> I work as Dave Howard's publicist. I'm sure you can understand that Dave is very busy and is unable to maintain one-on-one correspondence with his fans. So he apologises that he will no longer be able to correspond with you.
> Dave thanks you for your support and hopes that you continue to enjoy reading his work.
> Sincerely
> Jemima Taylor

What the …? I've just been given the brush off. I feel sick. I'm being treated like a stalker. I'm so embarrassed. And angry. I'm angry. Who does he think he is? I knew I shouldn't have said anything. I should never have admitted to going to that book-signing. I can't believe the tone of that email. Who do they think they are? These writers. I won't be treated like this. I'm not going to be treated like an overzealous fan just because I got a bit nervous when I met him. Just because I needed a chair. Fuck him. And his publicist. Fuck them both.

I start a new email to Dave Howard. I tell him what I think of him. I use the words arrogant and egotistical. I use them a lot. I tell him that he can shove this interview up his arse. That he is a prima donna. That he can't write for shit. Except that's not really true, so I delete it and write that it wouldn't kill him to wear a tie.

I press send.

I stare at my In Box. The number one is flashing at me.

I have one new message.

It's from Dave Howard. It's titled SORRY. It was sent two minutes ago.

Subject: SORRY
Date: Wednesday 2.43pm
From: DaveHoward@yoohoo.net
To: RachelHill@mymail.com.au

Rachel
Forgive me. I think your email address may have got caught up in a list of over-enthusiastic fans (mainly school kids) that my publicist had to send a friendly 'back off' email to. You wouldn't believe the stuff people send me. So ignore Jemima's email. Meanwhile I've been doing a phone interview for the last hour – but if you send through the questions now, I'll type up my answers ASAP. I signed one of your books? I think I actually recognise your name from *Escape* magazine. I remember the story you did on Dublin's literary pub-crawl.
Dave.

OHMYGOD.

OHMYGOD.

OHMYGOD.

He'll be reading my email right now.

OHMYGOD.

I log off. Breathe Rachel. Breathe. Think clearly. What to do. What to do.

My mobile phone starts ringing.

I don't want to look.

It keeps ringing.

I pick it up. The display says DAVE HOWARD. Why did I store his name in caps? It makes me feel like my mobile is screaming his name at me.

DAVE HOWARD IS RINGING YOU AND HE'S REALLY PISSED, it yells at me.

Ring ring. Ring ring. Ring ring.

ARE YOU DEAF? IT'S DAVE HOWARD. DAVE HOWARD IS RINGING YOU, my mobile phone screams.

Shut up, I want to yell at my phone. Stop yelling at me.

It stops. Thank God. I sit down.

It starts ringing again.

Ring ring. Ring ring. Ring ring.

IT'S DAVE HOWARD AGAIN. HE WANTS TO TALK TO YOU, says my mobile, this time a little more calmly, seductively.

'Hello?'

Rachel? It's Dave Howard.

'No shit.'

Excuse me?

'Oh fuck.'

Are you there?

'Maybe.'

I got your email.

I say nothing.

So, you think I should wear ties more often?

'Look Dave, Mr Howard, Sir, shit look, I'm so sorry. I don't know what's wrong with me. I'm so sorry. I just thought that you were giving me the brush-off because I was a fan. Because I went to a book-signing. I haven't been well lately. I've been stressed. I've had scurvy.'

Scurvy? Right. Realising that's about vitamin C of course. Sure. Well, why don't we just forget about it? It's my fault that your name got caught up in that list by accident. So, it's forgotten.

'Yes, yes that would be good.'

Okay.

'Okay.'

So just email me through the interview questions and I'll do them right now. How does that sound?

'Great. Wonderful. Great. Thank you. Thank you.'

I hang up.

I take a few deep breaths and go back online. Calm Rachel. Calm. I start a new email. I am exceedingly polite and professional. I attach the file with the questions about Dave's new book, *Perfect Summer*. I press send.

I go and make myself a scotch and dry.

Zoë rings.

So have you read it?

'What?'

My new piece of writing.

'What?'

Hello? My latest bit of writing. My latest erotic fiction entry?

'No, I haven't read it yet, Zee. Hang on.' I walk over to

the computer with the phone and sit down at the desk. 'What did you call it?'

Philomena Sequel. I haven't come up with a proper title yet.

I scroll down the list of files.

'I don't see it, Zee. Are you sure you saved it?'

Oh, no that's right. I used initials.

'Initials. Okey-dokey. There's no file called ZB here. Did you save it as a Word file?'

No, I didn't use my initials. I used the initials of Philomena Sequel. P.S.

And there they are in front of me. Two files. One called P.S. and one called PS. Both created today. Both created today but vastly different in content. My mouth starts to go dry. I go into my email account off-line. I find the email that I sent to Dave Howard. I click on the attachment. I start praying really, really hard that I emailed Dave Howard the right file. The interview questions. The file opens. I'm in deep shit.

I have emailed Dave Howard porn.

'I HAVE JUST EMAILED DAVE HOWARD PORN,' I scream to no-one in particular.

I pick up the phone. Zoë is still there.

WHAT?

'My interview questions were called PS – for *Perfect Summer*. I just emailed Dave Howard your porn story.'

By accident?

'Of course by fucking accident. Oh God. I'll have to phone him. Hope he doesn't open it. Tell him to trash it. I can't believe I just sent him porn.'

I'd really prefer it if you used the term "erotic fiction". Porn makes it sound so cheap.

I ring his number but it rings out. He must be on-line. On-line and reading porn. Fuck. I hang up the phone and go back on-line. I send him another email. I try to explain what happened, hoping he'll see the funny side. I attach the real interview questions. And then I wait. Staring at my email account. Feeling numb. Waiting for it. Waiting for the inevitable. Fifteen minutes later and it turns up. The email from Jemima Taylor. The email that tells me that my email address has been BLOCKED from Dave Howard's account. That I am not to contact him again. That what I have sent him is not only offensive but that she is also tempted to report me to the police.

I have a shower and go to bed. It's 5.38pm.

22

I'm a little distracted on Thursday morning since I didn't sleep well. I kept dreaming that I was playing Courtney Love's role in *The People vs. Larry Flynt*. Porn is beginning to take over my life. This overtiredness means that it's not until we're pulling up to Kenmore Primary School that I notice that Alex has smuggled Snowy in her school bag. I unzip her pink backpack and there's Snowy, looking up at me, wearing Alex's homework on his head like it's a beret.

'Alex, you can't take Snowy in with you.'

But he likes maths. Monsieur Snowy blinks up at me. He blinks like someone who could reel off prime numbers without hesitation.

'I know he does, but your teacher isn't going to want Snowy in the classroom with you all day.'

But Snowy misses me when I'm not there. He says that he has no-one to play with at big lunch.

'Well, he can sleep and eat his lunch. And he can think up all the fun games that he's going to play with you when you get home from school.'

But I have ballet this afternoon.

'No, today's Thursday. You have ballet tomorrow, Friday, silly-billy.'

Can Snowy come to ballet tomorrow?

'Maybe. What? No, I mean no. No, Snowy can't come to ballet. Look, Alex, the bell is about to go and you have to go inside. Off you go.'

Can you come and look at my work up on the wall? Mrs Healy has put our ant pictures up on the wall.

'Alex, I can't this morning. I have to get home. But I'll come tomorrow. I promise. I promise I'll come tomorrow.'

You never come. You never come and look at my work. Everyone else has someone what comes. Except me. No one ever comes to see my paintings.

'It's someone "that" comes, not "what" comes. And I will come. I'll come tomorrow. Snowy and I will come together.'

She says nothing. Instead, she climbs out of the car and I watch her trudge up to the school gates. She walks slowly, unenthusiastically. She walks sadly. Her school bag practically dwarfs her entire body. She looks small. Small and sad. Sometimes I forget that she's just a little girl. A little girl who likes drawing ants whose mum isn't around much to tell her how great those ants are.

I start the car. Snowy stares at me.

A little girl whose best friend is her narcissistic, beret-wearing cat.

Oh for God's sake.

'Alex!'

She turns around. Skeptical. Angry.

'Alex! Wait on. I'm coming. But you have to hold Snowy. Okay? You have to hold him while I look at your work.'

By the time Matt turns up for our 10am lesson, I'm already not in the mood. Possibly because I'm over-tired and stressed about the porn. Possibly because Snowy tried to sit on my head while I drove home in peak hour traffic.

You alright? asks Matt.

'Nope.'

He laughs. Until he sees that I am serious. *So, have you been practising?*

'Yes.'

Really?

'No.'

Okay, well this time, for something different, why don't you try playing the piece all the way through. Then we can see how far we've come. He raises his eyebrows and nods and for a few seconds I feel a twitch of attraction to him. Until I realise what he has just proposed.

'I'm not playing the piece all the way through. I've told you that before.'

Okaaaaaaay. So how about today's question. Ready? What is … the Mork and Mindy *theme song?*

'Very funny.'

Okay, today's question is, What song did Elton John write about the American actor Tony Danza?

'Tony Danza? Tony Danza from *Who's the Boss?*'

Yep.

'Elton John wrote a song about Tony Danza?'

Yep.

'What? No, he hasn't. You're making this up.'

Rachel, Rachel, Rachel … And Matt walks over to the portable CD player I have in the piano room, puts in an Elton John CD and presses track 5.

The next thing I know, Matt is singing "Hold me closer Tony Danza" to the chorus of Elton John's 'Tiny Dancer'.

'You are a fool.'

Okay, tough crowd this morning. I thought for sure that would make you laugh but you're right.

'So, that's today's question?'

Well, no. The real question is, in Growing Pains, *Jason and Maggie Seaver were the parents of … who?*

'Mike, Carol and Ben. And then Chrissy. Can we get started now? With the lesson?'

He pauses and looks at me for a moment. *So, what's wrong?*

'Nothing. I just want to get this done. I just want to learn this piece.'

Has something happened?

'You mean, apart from a cat sitting on my head and nearly making me crash my car this morning? Apart from that?'

Yeah, apart from the cat.

'No. Nothing's happened. I've just got a lot on my mind. A lot of things to do.'

Like what?

'Like, going to Coles and buying some real food tonight. Like getting a real job. Like learning this piece. Can we just get started please?'

Sure.

The hour passes slowly and we complete most of the lesson in silence. Matt just utters a few corrections here and there and that's about it. And that's okay. Right now silence works for me. Because some days when I talk to Matt it feels like we're rehearsing lines from a play. It's awkward and wooden and sorta fake.

You're really improving. I think you're totally on track to win this bet.

'Mmmm.' I start thinking about the blonde girl at his house. I want to ask him about it. I want to know who she is, just because Matt acts like he doesn't have any friends when, clearly, he does. Clearly, he is friends with a girl with blonde hair. A girl he feels the need to apologise to for something. I want to ask him. I must think of a subtle way to work it into the conversation.

'So, I saw a blonde girl leaving your house yesterday.'

The subtlety of a colonoscopy.

Yeah?

'Yeah.'

That's Fiona, he says. And he looks like he's going to say something else but the phone starts ringing. I turn and stare at it.

So, are you going to get that?

I look at Matt. I look at the phone. I look back at Matt.

'I just don't feel like talking to anyone.'

The answering machine clicks on.

Rachel, it's Karen. I've just had a call from Dave Howard's publicist. Something about porn. About you sending Dave Howard porn. God, I mean that just sounds ridiculous. I feel stupid calling you. I know that there's just been a misunderstanding. Anyway, give me a call back will you? Just so we can get this cleared up. Thanks.

I look at Matt. I can feel my face burning up.

He starts laughing and says, *You dirty dog.*

'Just leave!' I say to him. 'Will you just go?' And I can't look at him and I can feel my cheeks going red and my eyes start to go a bit wet. And all I can think about is how embarrassed, humiliated I am. Karen thinks I sent Dave Howard porn. I *did* send Dave Howard porn. I want to die. I grit my teeth and close my eyes and point towards the front door and say 'I can't deal with you right now. Just go.'

You were a Prefect at school, weren't you? I can tell.

'Matt!'

And I bet that you're one of those people in an office who acted as the Fridge Police. I bet you sent around the nasty email chastising everyone else about the dodgy food and old containers.

'Matt!'

And he walks out the front door laughing.

23

When I see Alex appear from her classroom at three pm I can tell that it hasn't been a good day. She opens the car door and I say, 'What's happened?' And her little face starts to crumple up and the tears begin to fall as she tells me that she was the only girl in 2A not invited to India Heath's Barbie Party and that she really wants to go. So could she just turn up?

'I don't think so,' I say.

Please?

'I don't think so.'

We sit in the car and I squeeze her hand when she tells me that the kids at school were mean today and she spent "big lunch" alone.

'Well, I've got a surprise for you.'

What?
'We're going to my house for a swim.'
Really?
'Yes. Absolutely.'
Is Mum coming?
'No, Mum's working late. Until five pm. So I thought it would be just you and me and some chocolate cupcakes that I bought especially for you.'
Can I have a Strawberry Quik at your house?
'You certainly can. I brought the tin with me. See? There in the backseat.' She turns around and sees it, sitting on top of her towel and swimsuit.

Alex spends an hour splashing around in the swimming pool and when she comes in, I'm on the phone to Jan from the Miss Brisbane Awards. Jan is trying to convince me to hold a car-rally with another entrant. She's worried I won't raise the $500 to qualify for the semi-finals.

I try to calm Jan down and convince her that I have everything under control. But that doesn't work, so I just say 'Gotta go!' and hang up on her instead.

Alex looks at me suspiciously.
Are you Miss Australia?
'No, Alex! I'm an entrant in the Miss Brisbane Awards …'
Are you? Her eyes go wide and her jaw drops open. *Are you going to be Miss Brisbane?*
'No, no, no I haven't raised enough money. The winner is the person who raises the most money.' Which isn't exactly true but it will have to do.

Why haven't you raised enough money?

'I don't know. Um, because it's hard.'

Why is it hard?

'Hey, do you want a chocolate cupcake and a strawberry milkshake?'

When Alex finishes eating her afternoon tea, I realise that it's after five pm.

'I think I'd better take you back home to mum.'

But I don't want to go home. It's boring at home. I want to stay. Please, Rachel?

So I phone Sharon and ask her if I can keep Alex with me until seven pm. That I'm about to do the grocery shopping and that I could really use someone to push the trolley. Alex nods excitedly as Sharon informs me that Alex is a wonderful trolley driver and that as long as she's not being a nuisance I can keep her with me while I do the groceries. I pass the phone over and the two of them chat briefly for a minute or two and I clear away the afternoon tea dishes, listening to snippets of conversation about ants and ballet shoes and the Miss Brisbane Awards and what it was like being on the surfboard in the pool. I hear nothing about India Heath or her Barbie party.

As I lock the front door, I read over my shopping list and mentally debate whether I have forgotten to write anything else down. Alex walks ahead of me and goes out to the car.

Rachel! There's a boy sitting on the fence.

'What?'

Look!

I turn around. And, she's right. There's a boy sitting on the fence, next to our letterbox. It's Matt.

I walk up to him.

'If I throw a stick will you go away?'

Nope.

Alex marches up to him. *Why are you sitting on the fence?*

I'm bored. Matt shrugs his shoulders.

Oh. She considers this for a while. *I'm Alex.*

Hello, Alex, nice to meet you. He hops off the fence. *I'm Matt. Rachel's best friend.*

'You are *not* my best friend.'

Isn't she grumpy? She's always so grumpy, it's a wonder I'm her best friend at all.

I shake my head and roll my eyes.

What are you going to do now? says Alex, hands on hips, her eyes wide.

Well, I was hoping that Rachel would take me grocery shopping tonight. My car won't start.

We're going grocery shopping right now. At Toowong Village! she pipes up.

You're going to Toowong Village? says Matt. *Do you think that I could come grocery shopping with you and Rachel?*

'Look Matt, usually I would give you a lift but after we do the groceries I have to go to David Jones. And then I have to drop Alex home. So we're going to be out for a while.'

Sounds good to me. And he winks at Alex and says, *So Alex, what do you know about* Mork and Mindy*?*

As soon as we walk through the turnstile at Coles I realise

what a mistake I have made going shopping with Heckle and Jeckle. At first, as we choose a trolley together, it feels as if we're some kind of weird little family unit. Me, Matt and Alex. Until Matt and Alex start on a medley of songs with the word "poo" in them. When they start on a Grease Poo Megamix (including Poo's The One That I Want, Hopelessly Devoted to Poo and Poo Lightning), I decide enough is enough.

'Will you two stop it?'

But this just makes it worse. They look at me with angelic, butter-wouldn't-melt-in-their-mouths expressions before exchanging mischievous glances. As if they're part of some cool club and I — well I'm just not.

The next fifteen minutes we're shopping peacefully. Too peacefully. They're too quiet. And that's when I notice the packet of nappies in my trolley. And the cake tins. And the rather large watermelon. And the colouring-in pens. And the Disney lunchbox.

'Right. That's it. This is taking twice as long as it should. Will you two just please stop …'

Sorry Rachel, says Matt, nudging Alex.

Yeah, sorry Rachel, says Alex, sucking in her cheeks, trying to suppress a laugh.

It's just that we love shopping at … POOwong! says Matt and they both start laughing again.

'Poowong. Yes, that's hysterical. I've got to go to DJ's and I'm beginning to get a headache. So can we all be calm for a while?'

We walk to David Jones in silence. Thankfully Alex is

getting tired and Matt, realising that I'm not in the mood for any more joking around, offers to take her into the toy department while I look for an engagement present for Angus and Claire.

I go up to the third floor, to the homeware and china departments – the adult departments. I walk around near the counter, wondering where the shop assistant must be. They all seem to be tied up. But despite the two delinquents waiting for me in the toy department I'm in no hurry. I wander around the Royal Doulton plates and the crystal vases and the sterling silver sugar bowls and I notice a young woman across from me. She looks about my age. She has blonde frizzy hair and is wearing a polo shirt and shorts. She's average looking. Not beautiful. Not ugly. Just average. I find myself trying to see her left hand. She's holding up a rather hideous platter. I strain my neck and there it is, her left hand in full view. No ring. She's not wearing a ring. For a moment, I feel better. Like I've found someone else on my team. Someone else who is still single, who has yet to find "them". That lid to every jam jar, as Patricia would say.

I've been doing this a lot lately, I've noticed. When I'm out doing the shopping or waiting at the school gates for Alex or waiting in line at the post office. I've become obsessed with looking at other women's hands, looking for a ring. It's a stupid game. Usually it depresses me. Because on the days when I spot a girl who I think is border-line ugly, a girl with greasy hair or horse teeth or bad dress sense and then I see the gold band glistening on her finger, I actually feel physically sick. Like I've taken a blow to the stomach. I want to scream out, 'How come YOU'VE found someone and I haven't?' But the announcer in my head says, 'Game Set and Match to the Married Woman. She wins.' Because despite her hair or her teeth or her leopard print jumpsuit, she still found someone. Someone out there loves her more than anything else in the world. She's been a bride. Unlike you.

I was never a bride. I got married in shorts and a T-shirt and I never wore a wedding ring and I never had a bridesmaid and I never had a gift registry or a honeymoon or wedding presents. And now I'm about to get divorced. And I never got to be the bride to begin with. I get the black mark against my name but I never got the fun stuff. The presents, the attention, the dress. The bit where you got to tell people you were married.

I really, really want to find a sales assistant and get this whole engagement present thing out of the way. I walk around the department and find myself walking past a small office. There's a woman behind a desk talking to two people. It looks like a staff meeting or even a job interview. And then, as I keep staring at them, and I see the young woman put her hand on the guy's leg, I realise that it's an engaged couple. How stupid am I? Of course it's a bloody engaged couple. Making a gift registry. And I stand there and just watch them flipping through a catalogue on small appliances and I wonder, What does she have that I don't have? What did she do right? Because some days, that's how it feels. It feels like I'm being punished and I just want to know what that girl in the room there did or said in order for someone else to love her so much they wanted to marry her. I continue to stare at this girl, hoping that I will notice what it is that she's got. The things she's got that I'm so clearly lacking.

Young lady, are you planning to buy those salad servers?

'What?' I spin around only to be greeted by Matt looking a little sheepish.

Rach, I'm sorry. He starts laughing. *The look on your face! I'm sorry, I didn't mean to scare you.*

'Where's Alex?'

Oh, well, she's over by the Peter Rabbit stuff. Hey Alex! he calls out across the shop. She comes running over and jumps into Matt's arms.

Rachel, guess what? Matt's gonna come to my ballet concert!

24

The atmosphere in the car on the way home is a little tense. Not that Alex notices. She sits in the back with Matt and just chats away to him about school and Snowy, and is he married and where does he live and does he like cats and how did he get that scratch on his neck and can he draw ants and a thousand other things that she never talks to me about. I can feel myself getting annoyed. Annoyed that these two have become so close, so quickly. Annoyed that Alex is sharing stuff with Matt that she has never shared with me.

When we get to Sharon's I introduce her to Matt. Even barefoot, in stonewash denim shorts and a paint-splodged man's shirt, Sharon looks beautiful. She pushes the stubborn blonde wisps out of her eyes and shakes hands with Matt before padding off into the kitchen with the assumption that we will automatically follow. Sharon and I talk the way we always do, with me occasionally explaining things to Matt so that he has some hope of keeping up. Meanwhile, I try to ignore the nudge-nudge-wink-wink subtleties that come from Sharon as she gives Matt the once over when he's not looking.

Yum! she mouths at me when Matt goes to check out Alex's room. *He's gorgeous!* But I roll my eyes and act repulsed. He's not gorgeous. He's a pain. A pain that eats all my almond bread. And then she nudges me and says, *And what's this about you being in Miss Brisbane? Alex says they're firing you for not raising enough money.*

And just when I finish explaining to Sharon that I won't be eligible to go through to the next round, Matt comes back out holding hands with Alex. When the discovery of Sharon's CD 'Spike' on the kitchen table prompts Matt and Sharon to start talking about their mutual love of Elvis Costello, I slip into the spare room to take a peek at Sharon's latest painting before returning to the kitchen where I decline the offer of a cup of coffee.

'We'd better head off. I'll catch up with you soon, Sharon. Bye Alex. Thanks for coming over.'

But Alex ignores me and says, *Bye Matt,* running over to him and giving him a giant hug. Sharon rolls her eyes.

Alex! Now say thank you to Rachel for letting you come over to her house. Because it was very nice of Rachel to let you come over and have a swim, wasn't it?

Alex rolls her eyes back at Sharon and then looks up at

me and says, *Thank you Rachel, bye Rachel,* in her monotonous robot voice that tells me I am the human equivalent of homework on a Friday afternoon.

And then I'm back in the car. Alone. With Matt. A regular Charles in Charge.

The seven-minute car ride home is uneasy. I'm pissed off. Which means that we make ridiculous angry small talk about Sharon and Alex, about my preference for Flora margarine, about how economical my Mazda is, but the conversation strains like a car engine being flooded.

And then we're pulling up into the driveway of my house.

'Here we are,' I say. And we both just sit there staring straight ahead, not making the slightest move to unclip our seat belts. I'm feeling annoyed and yet the tension between us is more than that. It's more than the pissed-off vibe I'm desperately trying to put out. There's something else that's making this awkward. Like the fact my heart feels like it's literally in my throat. This is ridiculous. I unclip my belt.

'So, look thanks for coming,' I end up saying to the windscreen wipers.

Matt says nothing. I look up at him. He's staring at me. Suddenly everything is quiet and I can feel the intensity level in the car going up a notch. My heart is thumping in my chest. I can hear Matt's breathing. Our eyes are locked. Even the radio DJ seems to stop talking to see what's going to happen.

Rachel.

I watch as Matt's left hand comes up towards my face and strokes my hair, his eyes never once leaving mine.

I can't do this.

'What the hell are you doing?' I push his hand away.

Rachel, you had a leaf in your hair. I was just trying to pick it out. He uncurls his hand and reveals a small brown crumply traitor-ish leaf.

Oh.

You seriously need to chill out.

'Look, I thought you were making a move. I thought you were doing the whole "brush her face in the car" thing. I just don't need this right now.'

Who said I was even interested in you? And if I was, I'm not stupid, Rachel. Anyone can see that to get to first base with Rachel Hill you need to put blonde tints in your hair, wear a Choose Life T-shirt and boast a questionable relationship with Andrew Ridgeley.

'Real funny.'

So …

Garbos come tomorrow, I must remember to put the bin out.

… Alex's ballet concert sounds like fun. When you were looking at Sharon's painting, she was telling me about her job at the station and the trouble she's having with her new boss and the pressure they're putting on her to do a later shift. I think she's worried that she's not always going to be able to pick Alex up from rehearsals …

I didn't know Sharon was having trouble with her job. How come he knows this? I can feel myself getting tense again.

… so I told her that if she ever gets stuck and if you can't do it, well, that I'd step in. You know, and pick Alex up.

'Right, well, that's kinda my job. Picking Alex up. And anyway, it takes Alex ages to get used to a new person. And she can be a handful.'

Oh sure. You're right. I just know what it's like to be an only child, when you're desperate for some attention, for someone to play with, especially when your mother's busy working all the time. Do you get the chance to actually play with her very often? 'Cause I know ...

'That's not my job, Matt. My job is not to be Alex's new play-friend. My job is to make sure she doesn't set fire to Snowy or suffocate him with sequins and perfume on a daily basis. What is this, anyway? Now you're giving me childcare lessons?'

You're upset.

'No. Don't worry about it, okay? But here's an idea: how about we spend the rest of this evening apart, you know, just for something different.'

He turns from me and looks out the window. *So you think we're spending too much time together?*

'No, no I think it's great that every time I turn around you're on my doorstep. Ten days ago I didn't know you and now, well, suddenly, you're picking Alex up from ballet rehearsals for me and telling me that I don't know how to look after her.'

I didn't say that ...

'Yes. Yes you did. But don't worry. It's not like that's my job or anything. Or that I hardly know you. And Alex and Sharon hardly know you.'

I pause.

'You want to know how often I play with Alex? Well, I

want to know why you're around here all the time. It's like you're trying to get into my life. So what is it? Are you thinking I'll be an easy lay? What? Tell me! Because, you know what, I just don't get it. And I'm not comfortable with it. And I don't need it. I don't need another hassle in my life. I don't need you hanging around me all the time. You're not my bloody husband.'

And, realising what I just said, I stop as abruptly as I started, like a dead car battery. I need to get out of this car. Out of this argument. I look up through the car window at the jacaranda tree that Caitlin and I planted when I was six. The flowers are still in bloom. Caitlin always used to say that her tree had its purple hair on – like a grandma with a blue rinse.

But now's not the time to be thinking about the jacaranda. I stare back at Matt and in his eyes I see a soupy mix of hurt and anger and betrayal. A mixture that I hadn't noticed in the midst of my soliloquy.

And thank God for that, he says with a wry laugh, scratching his chin. He looks up and looks me directly in the eyes. But this time, it's far from warm.

You know what, Rachel Hill? You don't know anything about me. He says that last part slowly, each word falling thickly out of his mouth like it's a chunk of Christmas ham that's been sliced off with a knife.

He gets out of the car and walks away, leaving me alone to argue with the twilight sky. I realise that when I went to Woolworths, I didn't even use my map. I'd said that I was going to be a shopper with a map. I couldn't even get that right.

25

Lying on my bed I can't stop thinking about what Matt said to me. 'Thank God for that.' Thank God I'm not Rachel Hill's husband. Who'd want to be married to Rachel Hill? That's what he meant. And maybe he's right. Maybe that's what Troy started thinking. Realised what he got himself into. Who he was going to be stuck with 'til death us do part. So he got out. And here I am. I'm a divorcee. A twenty-seven-year-old with one failed marriage under her belt. I lie on my bed and wonder about the irony of it all. That I have always been someone who preached that they would get married once and that it would be for life. That I was someone who took marriage seriously. So seriously it seems that I let a minister in an Elvis costume perform the ceremony.

I'm not sure why I really did get married that day. I have my theories. But they're not as dramatic or passionate or funny as if I had a team of scriptwriters penning my dialogue and treating my life like the B-grade sitcom it has become. I got married because I thought I loved Troy. Because his working visa in Australia had expired and the only way he and I could be in the same city was if we were married. Our relationship had started to fray at the edges. But, you see, I had already told everyone that he was 'it'. This was 'the guy', 'the one'. I wanted to be married. Twenty-seven seemed like a good age to me to tie the knot. And Troy was exactly the type of guy I saw myself being married to. The type of guy people would expect to see with me. He was intelligent, funny, ambitious, good looking and successful. And I suppose that I wasn't prepared to have a failed relationship to my name. I was Rachel Hill, magazine Features Editor, honours graduate, golden girl. I could fix anything. So I guess that I thought marriage was the answer. If Troy and I could just be together again everything would be okay. I could make everything okay. Like old times. So I pressured, cajoled, hounded him about getting married. Told him that we didn't have to tell anyone. Told him that we could do it on the quiet and then announce our engagement in a few months time, when I had moved to the States to be with him. No one would have to know except him and me. And the Immigration department. By the end, he was more enthusiastic than I was. *This will be hysterical*, he used to say, as if we were going on a Disney ride and not entering a legal and binding contract.

So we did it. I took a work trip and met Troy in Vegas. We spent the first two days playing slot machines and going up and down in the lifts at the Luxor and eating $5 buffets. Then on the third morning, we got up and had breakfast and played some slot machines and talked about what a great time we were having and how much we loved Vegas. I casually mentioned that I should visit some chapels because I wanted to do a story on Getting Hitched in Vegas and he nodded and pretended not to know that my research was going to include us becoming man and wife. Then we jumped in a cab and Troy told the driver that we wanted to go to the County Court to get a marriage licence. Or maybe it was me. The driver looked at us in the rear vision mirror and said, *You two planning on getting married?* And I said, 'Oh no, we're just doing research for a story. I write for Australia's biggest travel magazine.' And Troy looked out the window and said that he'd forgotten to ring his brother.

We stood in queues and filled in forms and showed ID but it wasn't really until we pulled up to a chapel on our way back to the hotel that it dawned on me what we were doing. The thing that neither of us could even talk about. That's when I began to feel sick. Not just nerves or butterflies but sick in the stomach. And as the priest at the Little Silver Bell wedding chapel went over the package options, asking me if I wanted the free plastic photo album and the confetti for an extra $25, I can remember saying no – just give me the basics, bare minimum. But would I like the taped organ music?

Troy grinned and said *Go on – do it for a laugh, Rach,* but

I turned to him and said, I don't want to walk down the aisle, I don't want music, I don't want flowers, I don't want confetti, I just want to say the words and have the witness and go home. I should have backed out then. I should have realised that this wasn't something I wanted to do. That I should have at least gone home and thought about it some more. But I didn't. I went into the back room — the chapel they called it — and said my part of the script. With my fingers crossed behind my back. As if that would prove that I didn't mean it – that this was all just a game. And instead of saying 'I do' I answered 'uh-huh' and turned my head when Troy went to kiss me on the lips, so that instead he just grazed my cheek. In the cab on the way home neither of us spoke and the cab driver who had waited for us out the front said, *So did you do it?* And Troy answered, *No, we're just doing research for a story. No marriage here.*

I flew back to Australia. Troy went home to LA. Via email, over the next few months, we made the plans for my move to the US. We applied for interviews with Immigration so that I could get my green card. Months went by. I wanted to come out sooner but Troy kept saying that I should work for as long as possible, so that we'd have some money in the bank. But then I eventually got sick of waiting. I wanted us to be together. Or maybe I just wanted a reason to resign from my job. The "dream job" that everyone said I'd be mad to ever leave. So I resigned. That night when I came home from work after I'd told everyone that I was moving to the US to be with Troy, I got his message on my answering machine. The "don't quit, we've made a mistake" message. The "I think we should get a divorce" message.

I didn't tell anyone at work. Having given them six weeks notice I played along that I was still going to the US. I didn't want to disappoint them, although it was that much harder when their leaving presents were USA guidebooks and a new set of luggage.

And now I'm here. Babysitting. Living at Mum and Dad's. Wearing lots of clothes that feature elastic waistbands. Being a complete bitch to some guy next door who's just trying to be friendly.

I get up early on Friday and put in some extra practise on 'Jessica's Theme'. But Matt doesn't show up for our lesson.

Even though I know it's my fault, I'm a little annoyed. I refuse to let it ruin my day, though. I convince myself that I'm pleased. That this is the best thing. We have been spending too much time together and, frankly, I'm busy. Busy with chores like ... wheeling the wheelie bin out to the footpath. And if Matt happens to see me outside, he will see that I am far from hurt by our fight. He will see that I am busy ... moving wheelie bins.

It's when I'm out on the footpath dragging the wheelie bin along that I see her. Walking out of Matt's house. The blonde girl. She's ridiculously thin. There's no sign of Matt. Just her, walking down the path towards this car. This red Laser with one of those dicky Bad Girl stickers on it. This time I want a closer look at her. So I pretend to be concerned about some of Patricia's plants but in my mind I feel like Jaws and I wait for her to get nearer. Then, I see her feet.

'Morning,' I say, springing up from the shrubs. And she is startled, clearly not expecting someone to morph out of plants at this hour of the day. No ring. She shakes off her fright, smiles and says *Morning*. But I am hardly paying attention to that because I am staring at the bruise on her face.

26

When I get home from Alex's house on Friday afternoon there is a large package on the doorstep. I open it and find a packet of Tim Tams and a Classic TV Themes piano book. The note attached reads: *A few treats to make your day. How about video and pizza tonight at my place?*

I look at the signature and smile.

I ring Zoë at work.

'When did you drop this package around? And thank you, by the way.'

Work courier. So if anyone asks, you're about to book a twenty-day bus tour through Europe and the Tim Tams are actually airline tickets.

We agree that 7.30pm would be a good time for me to

visit Casa Budd armed with cheezels and as many Nicolas Cage videos as I can lay my hands on. Just because Zoë's gay doesn't mean she can't appreciate a simmering Cage in *Moonstruck*.

An hour into my arrival and Zee and I are talking all the way through *Moonstruck,* only stopping to watch the scene where Nick takes Cher to the opera.

Hey, she says with a mouthful of vegetarian thin pizza. *Can you give me a lift to Angus and Claire's party tomorrow night? I'm letting Megan borrow my car to go to the coast this weekend since hers doesn't have air-conditioning.*

'I totally forgot about that party,' I say, placing cheezels on each of my fingers and thumbs. 'I mean, I got them a present and everything but I just forgot that the party was on this Saturday. I totally don't want to go — there's going to be a heap of people there who I haven't seen since I split with Troy and I'm just not in the mood for the "How's Troy? I thought you were moving to LA?" conversation.'

You worry too much. It'll be fine — anytime someone brings that up I'll change the topic …

'To what?' I say, admiring my cheezel jewellery.

To isn't it creepy how much Claire's cousin looks like Pete Sampras.

'Oh my God she DOES look like Pete Sampras.'

I know, imagine having her as your bridesmaid …

'Not to say that Pete wouldn't cut a dashing figure in pink taffeta.'

Not to say he wouldn't be a shoo-in for catching the bridal bouquet.

'But there's no denying the girl looks like a chimp,' I say, sagely sucking cheezels off my fingers.

We watch a bit more of the movie and then, out of nowhere, Zoë says, *So how's the Matt thing? Married him yet?* I tell her about the fight we had and Fiona, the blonde friend with a bruised face. And how much time he spends with me and how good he is at playing the piano and how we talk about TV trivia and how much it pisses me off that Alex warmed to him immediately whereas it's taking me weeks to get her to even smile in my direction. And I tell her about his liking for almond bread, how most afternoons I can hear him playing the piano and how he can't remember the *Mork and Mindy* theme song.

Zoe starts humming it immediately.

'That's my girl,' I say proudly, giving Zoë a pat on the head.

But Zoë wants to talk about the blonde girl with the bruises. She starts asking me about Matt's temper and if I have ever seen him get angry.

'What are you getting at? Do you think he's hitting her?'

I don't know, I haven't even met the guy but all this stuff about apologies and scratches on his arms and neck and that blonde girl having bruises. And didn't you tell me that most nights you go to bed listening to some woman cry?

'Yeah, but that's Margaret.'

Who said it's Margaret? You don't know that. You just assumed it's Margaret. I bet it's bloody not Margaret. I bet it's this blonde chick. She's probably having the crap beaten out of her by Mr Harvey Keitel the piano-player next door.

I ignore this last comment and keep thinking about the notion that Matt is hitting some girl. I just don't see it.

'Yeah, but he doesn't come across as aggressive at all. You know sometimes when you get a vibe from guys who are control freaks or overly aggressive or something? Matt's not like that at all – he's the exact opposite of that. This is stupid.'

You should ask him.

'Oh right, like I'm going to say, "Hey Matt you don't happen to smack that blonde girl around do you?" Just forget it, I'm probably totally wrong. Matt hardly comes across as some aggressive macho guy. Anyway, he's not even talking to me at the moment so …'

I have SO got the solution. Next time you're in the car with him play Prodigy's 'Smack My Bitch Up'. Yep. Then see what he does.

'That's appalling …'

You're right. You'd have to spend $30 on the CD.

'Well, no, I meant …'

But, for $2 you could make him watch The Tina Turner Story *– watch his reaction to Tina having the crap beaten out of her by Ike Turner. I'll even shout you the vid.* And she tosses me a $2 coin from all the change sitting in her ashtray.

I shake my head at her and take the video off pause. Twenty minutes later and Zoë says, *Oh, I forgot to tell you some news I heard today.*

'Oh yeah, what?' I say, not taking my eyes away from *Moonstruck*.

Remember Lisa Armstrong?

'Nup.'

Come on, Lisa Armstrong, the school captain at St Monica's.

'St Monica's. I always thought that was the dumbest name. I really find it hard to believe that there was ever a Saint called Monica. All the Monicas that I've ever met, they weren't well-behaved. Think about Monica Lewis – she was like the anti-Christ.'

Rach. Lisa Armstrong? You remember her, right?

'Yeah, yeah.' When I was a prefect, Lisa Armstrong and I shared a love-hate relationship thanks to our rivalry in inter-school debating. The last I heard she was married with two little girls and earning a bomb as a chartered accountant.

'Don't tell me ... Lisa Armstrong is now the CEO of the Hong Kong Bank?' I roll my eyes.

Well ...

I look up at Zoë.

'What, is she getting divorced?' My eyes light up.

No, well, I mean, she was going really well with the bank. They just made her the Vice President of some division or something, I don't know, but ...

'Can you imagine how much money she must be on now?'

But, umm, apparently she separated from her husband last year and, um, there was some battle of custody for the children.

There's something about Zoë's tone that is beginning to make me feel sick in the stomach. I turn the television off and face her.

'Is she okay?'

Well, that's the thing. Last week she went out to her parents' farm out near...

'Dalby? Yeah, yeah, they had a farm out near Dalby. I remember that.'

Yeah, Dalby. Well, she took an overdose of drugs or something. I don't know. But she died. She killed herself. Lisa Armstrong killed herself last week.

When I get home there is a message from Jan on my answering machine, asking me to please return her call so that we can touch base about my fundraising plans. And whether I actually have any. I ignore this and go on-line to find two emails from Miss Brisbane entrants. One is asking for advice about her media release (I rewrite it for her and email it back) and the other wants some tips for a radio interview she is doing the next day about her fundraising (I write out a list of questions a journalist would usually ask and tell her to practise her replies).

And then I decide to spend some time Breaking in the Colt. And trying not to think about Lisa Armstrong.

27

On Saturday night we get a cab to Claire and Angus's party because I decide that I need a drink or two to survive the evening. Survive my old uni crowd. The crowd who thinks I'm still working on the magazine. Still with Troy.

We turn into Bank Street. The party is at Angus's parents' house in Chelmer. A big old Queenslander with a huge yard, a swimming pool and frangipani trees. As the cab pulls up outside the house, I notice that fairy lights have been strung up in the garden.

'I thought this was a low-key thing. Angus said it was just a BBQ. This doesn't look low-key. Fairy lights aren't low-key.'

But Zoë isn't listening. She's still yakking on and on about engagement presents. I consider telling Zoë that I will buy her $50 worth of drinks if she'll tell the cab-driver to turn around and head back out into the city. But Zoë's already handing over money to the cabbie and saying to me, *I'm fucked if someone else got them a touch-lamp.*

My fate isn't just sealed, it's been bolted down with a nail-gun. The only place I'm going is into that engagement party.

We walk through the garden and over to the marquee that has been pitched in the backyard and dump our gifts on the presents table. There are about fifty people here, mostly talking in their own cliques. I spot Angus's little brother Jason playing waiter with a tray of drinks. He sees us and immediately hands us two champagnes. I say, 'Jase, how did they rope you into this?' He just laughs and says, *Hey I'm Mr Alcohol, you need anything just let the old Jase-ter know.* I laugh out loud and say 'How's uni?' and he rolls his eyes and says, *Pretty shit.*

But then Angus calls out, *About bloody time* and I see him charging over to Zoë and I with a huge grin on his face.

I'm so glad you guys are here.

I smile awkwardly.

So, you guys are right for drinks, he says, nodding eagerly, looking at the champagne flutes in our hands.

I skull my champagne and say, 'Not really.'

She's soooo going to peak too early, Zoë says to Angus in disgust, shaking her head. *How many drinks did you have before we left the house?*

'Just one.'

Sure, just one ... bottle.

'Okay, fine, I had two glasses of wine. Big deal.'

Hmmmm.

But Angus smiles and says, *Who cares? Just have fun. Wait here, two champagnes coming up.*

What I didn't realise was that Angus meant two champagnes *each*. I manage to say hi to Claire without slurring any words but the truth is I'm a tad pissed within twenty minutes. But at least I have the dutch-courage to face my old uni buddies. Confronted with a constant stream of *How's Troy? I thought you were moving to LA?* comments, I start the evening off by telling people that Troy and I have decided to split because of divergent trans-Pacific career opportunities and that I am in fact writing my first novel. They nod and start asking my opinion on the latest Miles Franklin winner and my feelings on Arts funding. I start snatching up glasses of champagne from Jason like a games-show contestant grabbing one hundred dollar notes in a money vault.

Two hours, six champagnes, two VBs and the remaining contents of Jason's own personal bottle of Bundy Rum (which he offered to fetch from his bedroom cupboard) later, and I am the focus of a publishers' bidding war and have been issued an $80,000 advance. And I'm dating Bernard Fanning from Powderfinger. Things start to go a bit fuzzy. I laugh too loud at people's jokes. I laugh even louder at my own. Zee comes up and tries to take a glass of wine out of my hand. I respond by telling people that Zoë once thought the Bay of Pigs Invasion was a chapter in *Animal Farm*. To her credit, Zoë smiles as everyone laughs and she leads me away to get a glass of water, whispering into my ear, *I think you'd better slow down tiger, it's H2O time.*

But I don't want water. I'm feeling great. Great! I'm on fire. The life of the party. In the kitchen I grab the tablecloth off the kitchen table, wrapping it around my shoulders before grabbing a colander from the sink and placing it on my head.

'Watch me walk like Miss Brisbane. Watch me, Zee.' And I do my Miss Brisbane walk, which involves lots of pointy toes and regal waving around Angus's kitchen, and then out along the veranda all the time humming *Romper Room* songs about being straight and tall and not letting my basket fall. And then the colander falls off my head and Zee mutters, *Hill, you've got lettuce in your hair.*

And then I spot it. The beer that someone's left under a chair out near the hills hoist. That beer's mine. 'Mine. Mine. Mine.' I say out loud to Zoë. Zoë says, *I give up,* as I leave her in my dust, running down the veranda steps and diving for the beer commando-style. This warm beer in its slightly cracked plastic cup is the 'transition' drink. The drink where I move from the "I-love-youse-all" life of the party to the "nobody-loves-me/my-life's-screwed" depressed drunk.

Suddenly the world looks a lot more bleak. My head starts to spin. I lie down on the grass. I think about Lisa Armstrong. I think about how lonely she must have felt. How desperate things must have seemed. I look up. Most of the guests seem to have gone home. Angus's parents are clearing away plates and cups and serviettes. I don't feel like joining in. So, nursing my beer, I take up residence behind the brick BBQ at the back of the garden and start sobbing about Lisa. And about Troy. And then Jason finds me and says, *Are you okay?* and offers me some liqueur chocolates he just found in his father's study. So I pash Jason — who turns 18 in two weeks — telling him repeatedly that I think marriage is the destroyer of modern society. And would he mind very much if I called him Luis.

28

We had sex behind the BBQ. Apparently. According to Angus. And his somewhat startled mother who was wiping down the BBQ at the time. Fuzzy recollections swirl around in my head on Sunday as I lay in bed. I convince myself that Angus is teasing and that the "Jason Hours" never happened.

And then I feel the cobbler's pegs in my undies.

Sunday is a shit day. I haul myself out of bed at noon. I feel like crap. For the first time, I actually look like my passport photo. I drink water 'bubbler-style' from the bathroom tap and try to recall what happened to Zoë.

I vaguely remember that she resurfaced at eleven pm with smudged lipstick holding hands with Michelle, the Pete Sampras look-a-like bridesmaid. They were very smug with each other until Zoë, herself a tad pissy, introduced Michelle to me as 'the Pete Sampras look-a-like bridesmaid' – sending Michelle into tears and Zoë into an unnecessary diatribe about the future of Davis Cup tennis.

I head downstairs and notice the light on the answering machine is flashing. I hit play. Jason has left a message doing a dodgy Spanish accent, inviting me to Archerfield International Speedway next Saturday night. I'm not sure you're allowed to date someone that you once tutored in Year 10 Modern History.

29

On Monday morning, Alex talks constantly about Matt. I am forced to tell her that Matt has moved away and gone to live in Noirville (location of Sabine, my Grade Five French penfriend). I also mention in passing that, actually, if Alex had spent a little more time with Matt and been a tad more discerning with her friendship, she would have seen that he's not that funny. Not funny at all, really. And, not that I'm trying to make a big deal out of it, but Matt would never let her have seven teaspoons of Chocolate Quik, not like me. When it comes to Chocolate Quik, Matt's one tight bastard.

'See how fun I am, Alex?' I say, heaping chocolate powder into her glass like Nigella Lawson on speed. In return, Alex looks at me blankly, reapplies her lip-gloss and says that she needs to do a wee.

I get home at 9.05am and sit by the front door and wait for Matt. It's one thing for him to miss Friday's lesson but surely he wouldn't miss Monday's lesson.

By 11.13am I realise that he would dare to miss Monday's lesson. Fuck. I must have really really upset him. I sit tapping the tabletop with a pen. There's only one thing I can do to fix this. I go to the window closest to Matt's kitchen.

'Mork calling Orson, come in Orson. Mork calling Orson, come in Orson.'

Matt comes to the window. I notice that he doesn't have a shirt on. He appears to be in a pair of cut-off army shorts.

Yes?

He has a six-pack stomach.

Why are you staring at my stomach?

My eyes dart upwards. 'I'm not, I wasn't staring at your stomach. Why would I be staring at your stomach?'

Did you want something, Rachel?

'I'm totally bored and desperate for a piano lesson.'

He just stares back at me.

'And I'm sorry. About what I said. I didn't mean it. Really.'

I'll be right over.

And so everything returns to quasi-normal. Me at the piano playing sections of 'Jessica's Theme' trying hard not to think about Matt's stomach. Matt spreading almond bread crumbs through the lounge room and chastising me for playing too fast. I decide that I want to talk about our fight. But not now.

'So, I was thinking that maybe you could come over for dinner tonight. No big deal, just dinner – no biggie.'

Dinner would be great but there's one condition.

'Yeeeeees?'

I get to cook.

'Cool. What are you going to make?'

Not telling.

'What are you, five?'

Hey, I know what you're doing. You're trying to distract me from asking you that fifth question. Remember our bet last week? If you don't get this question right, you have to play me 'Jessica's Theme' all the way through.

'Fine, shoot.'

Okay, the fifth question is … on The Partridge Family, *what was the name of the family's agent?*

'Reuben,' I say confidently. 'Reuben … Reuben …' My mind is blank. I can't remember.

'Tate,' I blurt out. But I'm not entirely convinced. Actually, I think I'm wrong. I think I'm thinking of Larry Tate from *Bewitched*. Shit.

Matt throws his head back and does an evil laugh. *It was Kincade. Reuben Kincade. Alright sister, crack those knuckles, it's time to play this piece from start to finish.*

My heart starts beating out of my chest. I'm just not ready. It's not perfect yet. I stare at the sheets and wet my lips, swallowing nothing because my tongue feels like sandpaper. I try and steady my hands, all the while conscious of Matt watching me. I've got to pull it together.

And then Matt does something I wasn't expecting. He gets up from the couch and goes over to the front door.

Oh shit, Rachel, he says, looking at his watch, looking at me, looking back at his watch. *I totally forgot that I have to be somewhere right now. We'll have to do this some other time. I'm really sorry. I'll see you tonight for dinner, though. I'll be over at six-thirtyish.*

And Matt runs out the front door guilty of the worst acting I have ever seen. But saving my life.

30

I'm nervous. After nearly two weeks of Matthew Harding walking around my house, making jokes about my parents' furniture, scrutinising family photos, becoming overly familiar with the Hill family pantry – suddenly now I'm worrying about his opinion. This is because, to date, I have confined Matthew Harding to one section of the house. Tonight he will be sitting in the dining room having dinner with me. And for Matthew to get to the dining room, he will have to walk through the rest of Casa Hill.

I spend an hour getting ready. Doing my hair, squirting perfume, applying subtle makeup. I make myself a large scotch and dry. And then I practise making dinnertime conversation, like an adult. I practise throwing my head back and laughing in a charming manner. 'More wine, Matthew? Frankly, I think blame for the fuel crisis lies firmly in the lap of OPEC.' I have no idea what OPEC really stands for. Better to stick with topics I know. 'I've always found that the best time to travel to Cairo is September.' As I float around the house making conversation, the state of the house catches my eye. It's a mess. I must tidy. I assume Patricia's 'clean surfaces' mentality and start sweeping magazines, letters and other paraphernalia off benchtops and coffee tables and microwaves. I find lids for pens. I hide my hideous graduation photo and just leave Caitlin's Glamour Shots one. I hide Caitlin's graduation photo. I walk into the formal lounge room and notice Patricia's crochet magazines. I dump them behind the stereo. Which turns my eyes to my parents' CD collection.

I'm fucked.

The entire CD tower is filled with Judith Durham, Andy Williams, Kenny G and ELO. This is what happens when you live with your parents, you run the risk of being associated with their dress sense, their CD collection and their obsession with *Heartbeat*.

I snatch up as many offending CDs as I can hold and then the phone rings.

It's Louise – one of the Miss Brisbane entrants. At eighteen, Louise is the youngest entrant and has emailed me twice this week already with media questions.

Rachel? I'm so sorry to ring you at home but I've got to do an interview with my local Quest paper early tomorrow morning. And I'm just really nervous.

'What are you nervous about in particular?'

I'm worried that I'm going to say the wrong thing. You know? Make a mistake. They're doing a story on the quiz night I'm holding next weekend. They're trying to help me sell tickets and stuff. But I'm just worried that I'm going to stuff up.

'Okay. This is not a big deal, Louise. Really. And those Quest journos, they're lovely. It's not like it's *Sixty Minutes*. The *North-West News* is not going to try and get any dirt on you.'

Yeah, I s'pose, she laughs.

'So, if it were me, I'd type up a list of the key points I'd want to mention in the interview. And then you can have that in front of you when you're on the phone. And they'll never know. See? Then you can make sure you don't forget to mention the main points. And, why don't you offer to email them or fax them through a list of the main details about the Quiz Night and also about yourself and the charity you're fundraising for.'

The Royal Flying Doctor Service.

'Yeah, the Royal Flying Doctors. Email the journalist some key information about them. And that's a good way to make sure they get all the information they need.'

Yeah. Okay, that sounds good. I'm really sorry to bother you about this. I just needed some tips. I feel much better now, though.

There's a knock on the front door. Matt.

'Not a worry, Louise,' I say walking over to the front door to open it. 'I gotta go, though, so good luck.'

And then I put the phone down and open the front door for Matt.

181

Hey, he says, grinning.

'Hi.'

So, what do we have here?

I have forgotten that I am still carrying around my parents' CDs. The CDs that can only hurt me. I want to turn. Run. Hide. But it's too late. Matt has spied the *Greatest Movie Theme Songs on Panpipe* that is on the top of the pile in my arms.

Ahh, the old Panpipe Greatest Hits. That's what I like about you, Rachel Hill – you don't limit yourself to the bad music of any particular decade. You give all of it a go.

And I say, 'Just shut up and come inside.'

There's no point trying to hide the CDs now, so I dump them on the lounge and try to see the funny side. Meanwhile, Matt has decided that tonight's dinner soundtrack should be chosen by him. So he makes me stay in the kitchen while he goes to choose the least crappy CD in the collection. Minutes later and I'm hearing Frank Sinatra's 'Witchcraft'.

'Hey, this is a great song,' I call out. 'Frank rules.'

Matt re-enters the room singing the chorus to me, using a lemon Ruski as a microphone before handing me a drink.

Now, I need a wok, some sharp knives and a high maintenance, volatile girl to talk to while I cook. Do you think you could arrange that for me? I roll my eyes. *And no looking at my arse when my back is turned.*

'You're an idiot.'

I go and fetch Patricia's chopping board and as I pass it to him, his hand touches mine. Just for a second. But the effect is like an electric shock. I flinch and my hand retracts immediately like a tape measure being snapped back up.

'I'll get out of your way,' I say quickly. 'The wok's down there, in the draw under the stove.'

Before I know it, Matthew Harding is in my kitchen chopping, stirring, peeling and blanching a range of fresh ingredients. I'm still not sure what we're having but I sit cross-legged on the kitchen bench, drinking my way through some lemon Ruskis and talking to him while he prepares our evening meal.

'I've never really known how to chop up tomatoes,' I blurt out, instantly regretting what I've just said. He looks up at me and says, *Come here.*

'No, I really don't ...'

Come. Here.

I climb down from my benchtop position and stand next to him at the sink.

He stands beside me and says, *The most important thing to remember is that you've got to hold the knife at this angle. And then it's just a downward motion, like this. See? Not too thick.* I have a go and end up butchering the vegetable so it is unrecognisable and looks instead like pulp.

Here, he moves behind me and puts his hand over mine. *It's easy, just do it like this.* I can feel his breath on my hair and the touch of his hand is giving me butterflies in my stomach.

At 7.10pm Matt and I are in the kitchen cooking dinner together and getting mildly drunk.

At 8.10pm Matt and I are sitting in the waiting room of the Taringa Medical Centre, Matt holding a blood-soaked tea-towel around his left hand and me apologising over and over in a slightly pissed fashion.

'Would you like a glass of water?' I say, grabbing his good hand and looking into his eyes earnestly. Any prior fears about touching Matt are out the window – suddenly I am the Queen of touchy-feely.

No, it's okay.

'Does it hurt? I never wanted to hurt you. Just because we fight doesn't mean that I want you to have glass in your hand. I'm not like that.'

Nah, it's not that bad. Looks worse than it is. He smiles.

'Do you hate me now? Do you wish that you never met me? Do you wish that you lived on Sesame Street? Grover would never drop a glass on the floor.'

Hill, it's fine. Trust me.

'He doesn't even have ears. Grover, not you. You have ears.' I stare at my own left hand. 'Where do you think they will put the stitches?' I look at my palm. 'I can see a big M on my palm for marriage,' I say to myself but loud enough for everyone else in the room to hear. Loud enough for the uni student near us to mutter, *Pity it's not an S,* for shut the fuck up.

Matt takes my hand in his. He slowly turns my hand over so it is palm up. *I think that they'll probably put some stitches in along here.* And he traces a path down my palm. He stops briefly and then continues tracing his finger down my wrist and up to my watch.

'Oh,' I say staring at my hand.

Rachel?

I look up and Matt is staring at me. The way he did in the car on Thursday night.

'Oh Matt, Matt, Matt,' I say, pulling my hand back. My head is spinning. 'Did you know that when I kill spiders I spray them until they go white. Like it's snowing.'

Well, I think …

'Matt, you know what, I know that I look like an under-achiever but I'm not. I was the Features Editor of a magazine. You know that's impressive. Rebecca Gibney's never been a magazine editor.'

No, but I don't think …

'I'm smart, Matt. I'm an achiever. A winnerrrrrrrrrrrrrr. You know Myers-Briggs? I did really well in that. I'm a Field Marshall. That's the top. The best you can get. So I won.'

You know, I don't think there's a right or wrong with Myers-Briggs. I don't think you can "do well".

'No,' I say, grabbing Matt's good hand. 'You're wrong. You can. Belieeeeeeeeeve me. And I'm an achiever.'

And then I fall off the lounge and onto the floor.

Here you go, champ, says Matt, helping me back up. *I'll get us both a magazine.* Matt walks over to the cane basket, which is home to ripped and coverless editions of every women's magazine ever printed. He picks up two magazines and offers me a choice. But I let Matt have the most uncrumpled copy with the story on Robbie Williams and Geri Halliwell. It's the least I can do, since he's injured and all. I stare down at my *For Me* magazine and start thinking about how we got here. Everything was going fine for the first half hour or so. Somehow I told Matt about my entry in the Miss

Brisbane Awards. I told him how I have to nominate a charity to raise money for. I suggest Red Cross, Amnesty International or maybe the RSPCA. Matt suggests something a little less obvious, something with a smaller profile like the Alzheimer's Association or even the Blue Care Nurses.

We debated this for a while, him munching on raw green beans and snowpeas, me drinking scotch and drys in rapid succession. Somehow we got onto the topic of our favourite TV shows. I started talking about my favourites and we agreed on all of them except *Mother & Son*, which Matt hates. He thinks it's derogatory. As I grabbed some wine glasses out of the cabinet, Matt said, *I think* Friends *went downhill after that stupid Rachel and Ross Vegas wedding. It's so implausible.*

I dropped the wine glasses onto the floor.

I swung around and looked at him, searching his face for clues. To see if he knew what I had done and was making some kind of jab at me and my predicament. But there wasn't. He couldn't possibly know.

So that's how we came to be sitting in the Taringa Medical Centre. Matt bent down to pick up the pieces of glass and promptly cut open his hand. While I grabbed another drink, muttered apologies and explained away the accident by saying that I lost grip for a moment.

Matt said I looked like I'd seen a ghost. But, in reality, I don't know what shocked me most. Hearing the words "Vegas wedding" come out of Matt's mouth or hearing his negative opinion on the whole Elvis wedding scenario. Everyone's a critic.

Eight o'clock on a Monday night and the Medical Centre isn't as busy as I'd thought it would be. Just a few school kids and their weary parents, an old woman with a bandaged foot and a uni student who looks like a flea carrier. We sit on the big leather couches, me trying to sober up and Matt reading the magazines and half watching the TV that has the sound turned down. But even in my slightly inebriated state I still notice the reaction to Matt. The staff here know him. Some say hello by name, others give a 'hey how are you?' smile or a nod when they see him sitting with me.

'How come everyone here knows you?' I ask, yawning, as we wait our turn for Matt's name to be called.

I'm accident-prone, can't you tell! He gives a half-hearted laugh and goes back to reading the magazine on his lap. I realise that for the first time since we met, I don't believe him.

In the cab on the way home I am practically asleep on Matt's shoulder, while Matt nurses four stitches in his left hand. When the cab pulls up, Matt pays and we're standing out on the road doing the awkward end of the night conversation. I invite Matt round for a video tomorrow night, to make up for tonight's disastrous dinner.

What are we going to watch? he asks.

'Dunno. But I've always wanted to watch *The Tina Turner Story*,' I reply cautiously, watching his reaction. But there is none.

★ ★

I'm not functioning at my best on Tuesday. I'm battling a hangover. All I ever wanted to be was an enigma. But I'm pretty sure enigmas don't get drunk and tell people they like to do 'secret wees' in the ocean.

Matt arrives at seven pm, with his bandaged hand and a bottle of wine.

'Oh, look, I don't really think I should be drinking tonight,' I say.

It's sparkling apple juice, Hill, no need to panic.

'Hmm, I think I'll be sticking to water.'

You're the boss. Field Marshall.

'So, what do you want on your pizza?'

Nothing that's ever appeared in a tin of fruit salad.

'Okay.'

The night goes well. Better than well. No one is injured. When Matt spies a Snakes and Ladders board game hidden at the back of the TV cabinet, he insists on a quick match before we start the video.

I thrash him. Six times.

I can't believe that you beat me every time. I can't believe it. I hate this game. It is a bad, evil game designed to destroy self-esteem.

'Does losing make you angry?' I say slyly.

No. Why? he laughs, packing up the board and dice.

'Just wondering. No reason. You don't feel like, say, hitting anything? Don't just want to sort of punch something ... or someone?' I say, under my breath.

No! Why? Why are you asking me that?

'Oh, I'm just curious – I just remember that you said to

me that you had your father's Irish temper. So, you know, just curious.'

Definitely time for the video. We settle back on the couch and start the three-hour marathon that is *What's Love Got To Do With It? – The Tina Turner Story*.

Six hours later and I wake up on the couch with a blanket over me. The TV has been switched off. Matt's nowhere to be seen. I look at the clock – it's 3.08am. There's a note stuck to the TV.

Hill, you were asleep within the first thirty minutes. Thought we could watch this another time.
Matt
P.S Nice snoring
P.P.S Snakes & Ladders sucks

31

When I arrive at Alex's house on Wednesday morning I find her in the front garden in her white cotton nightie wheeling her pink pram around the lawn. The pram has seen better days – Alex has stuck stickers all over the wheels and the paint is beginning to peel so that the pram resembles a snake trying to shed its skin. But Alex doesn't notice or doesn't care. I walk over to her. She is talking into one of her building blocks, which I assume has transformed into a mobile phone.

'Hello.'

Alex looks up at me, slightly annoyed. Her hand covers the pretend mouthpiece of her brick-come-mobile phone. *Shhh, the baby's sleeping. So don't wake him up.*

'Sorry,' I say, a little too sincerely, considering that I am talking to a six-year-old in her pyjamas who's talking into a piece of wood. I peer into the pram to see which doll Alex has bundled up. Staring up at me is a rather disgruntled looking Snowy, dressed in one of Alex's Barbie T-shirts with an old floral bonnet jammed on his head. Snowy blinks up at me — blinking some kind of morse code SOS. In that get-up he has the street cred of Holly Hobbie.

I turn on my heel to head into the house but then I stop. I decide to stay outside with her for a while. To play. And that's exactly what we do. We pretend to be grocery shopping with me bumping into Alex in the cereal aisle, commenting that despite the facial hair and occasional fur ball, she does indeed have the most beautiful baby in the world. And then we sit on the grass and pretend to drink tea and talk about how much our babies cry and how many pooey nappies they have. I get grass stains on my shorts and a green ant bite on my foot but Alex seems so happy that I stay for another few minutes or so before going in and making her some scrambled eggs.

As soon as I walk into the house when I get home, the phone is ringing. It's Sharon.

Rachel, guess what? You know Maggie, that I work with?

'Um yeah, I've heard you mention her before.'

Well, Maggie's husband's brother knows the guy who owns the RE. So, I've arranged for you to collect donations at the RE on Thursday night. Tomorrow night. All you need to do is get a group of friends together and some collection tins and I'm sure you'll collect at least five hundred dollars. The more drunk they are, the more generous they are. This way, you're still in with a chance to qualify for Miss Brisbane. How does that sound?

'Well ...'

I just felt bad because, you know, you'd probably be able to raise the money if you weren't running around after Alex all the time. Doing extra hours for me. So, what do you think? About taking donations at the RE?

And I say the only thing I can say. I say, 'Thanks, Sharon. You're a lifesaver.'

Matt doesn't come over for any lessons today. I realise that, unofficially, our lessons are over. Officially, his left hand has been shredded. Not that he used it that much during lessons. It was me that was playing, not him. But he's still not coming over. When we talked about it last night, I insisted that he stay home and rest. He'd tried to convince me that we should keep going but no, I said. Secretly, I hoped that he would refuse to take no for an answer. Just turn up. Miss me. But here I am sitting at the piano practising alone. 'Happy Frog' stares up at me forlornly, desperately wanting to knife Jessica or spook her horse so that he can go back to being in the spotlight. But I have moved far beyond the cha-chaing amphibian. Thanks to Matt. With the volume turned down, I play and play and play and it occurs to me that I am making far fewer mistakes and that I can practically play the piece by heart. And it sounds okay. Not brilliant but okay. Better than it did two weeks ago. This is good. I'm in control. I think again about the Miss Brisbane Awards. And the Dave Howard porn incident. And the fact that I'm unemployed and married. But all is not lost. I can either drown or keep swimming. I've got to keep swimming. Keep going. Stay in control.

I go to the fridge and get the divorce papers out of the dairy compartment. I let myself sign them all bar one page. I put them back to chill alongside the too-hard butter. The dairy compartment has become the too-hard basket. Ha ha, I laugh to myself. Even divorcees have a sense of humour.

When I return to pick Alex up after school, I walk up to her classroom and stand outside and wait. Like the other mothers. Except they all know each other and they stand around in their bluest blue jeans and pinstriped shirts or their gym gear and talk about Clara's violin lessons and Anoushka's Tibetan yoga class and Charlie's Spanish tutor. While Clara and Anoushka and Charlie stand nearby and pick their noses and scratch their scabby knees waiting for their older siblings to come out of the Grade Two classroom. I look back inside to Alex's room. I don't often get to stand and watch her like this. Watch her sitting at her desk, concentrating hard on colouring-in something that looks like an owl. And then, as if she can sense me watching her as she colours, she looks up at the window and flashes a half-smile. I can't tell if she's pleased or annoyed. And then she does a secret mini-wave that Mrs Healy won't notice.

I grab her school bag from the outside rack and hand it to her when she comes running out.

'What's that?' I say, pointing to her artwork which, on closer inspection, I see resembles not an owl but a person standing near a car. A person with big glasses. And a hairstyle à la electrocution.

It's Mummy, she says, looking around. *It's Mummy on her way to school to pick me up.* She looks around to see if Sharon might be with me. As if her picture could will the scenario into action. But not today.

Why did you meet me up here? she says angrily, scrunching the picture into her school bag.

'I just thought that I'd surprise you.'

Oh, she says.

'Hey, gimme another look at that picture.'

It's dumb, she says, but she reaches into her school bag anyway and begrudgingly hands over the crumpled crayon drawing. I smooth it out and have another long look at her artwork.

'Mmmm. You know what I think? I think your Mum is going to LOVE this. And,' I say, squatting down so that I am Alex's height, 'I am constantly amazed by your fabulousness.'

She grins and starts to giggle.

'Now let's go home and show this masterpiece to Snowy.'

As we start walking to the car, Alex's hand reaches up and grabs hold of mine.

32

You*'ll have to do my zip up – where are you? Come out!*

I tuck the strands of hair under the black material and survey the results in the mirror. I look like a dick.

'I'm not coming out.'

I look hot. This outfit totally suits me. I look just like Josephine Byrnes in Brides of Christ.

'Nuns aren't supposed to look hot.'

Come on, Sister Mary Clarence, out you come.

I walk out from behind the changeroom curtain. Zoë is admiring herself in the mirror. *I always wanted to be a nun*, she muses, swishing her habit back and forth.

'You did not. You always wanted to be a mortician.'

I'd be a great nun. I totally suit the uniform.

'Pity about all that "Thou shalt not covet thy neighbour's wife, thou shalt not write porn" stuff, though. You'd do for the habit what *Allo Allo* did for the French Resistance.'

This is going to be so much fun. I'm telling you, Rach, we will collect twice as much money tonight dressed like this.

'I feel ridiculous.'

You should have a fancy dress for your birthday.

'Nup.'

You never do anything crazy …

'Do the words "Vegas" and "wedding" mean anything to you?'

Let me finish. You never do anything crazy for your birthday — you deserve to do something wild.

'I don't want to do something wild,' I adjust my wimple in the mirror. 'I want to do something low key, low stress. Zero effort. Like Angus and Claire's engagement party.'

Zoë stares at me, eyebrows raised.

'That was a joke. A joke. I'm not having a party.'

We'll make it "Come as your hero".

'Are you deaf?'

Oh God, says Zoë, slapping her leg before realising her gaff. *Sorry Father,* she says, doing a quick cross. *You just know that Angus will come as Julio Iglesias. I think he only does it so that he can sing 'To All The Girls I've Loved Before' on your karaoke machine — and wear gold chains and open shirts. And he'll be speaking in a Spanish accent, which means, of course, that you're bound to end up having sex with him. Have you heard from Jason?*

'Bugger off. I'm not having a party,' I turn around in the

mirror looking at myself from different angles. At least black is slimming.

You're just grumpy because you can't think of anyone to come as. You don't have a hero. I know what I'll do. I'll pray for you. Pray that you find a hero.

'Whatever.'

I'm going to come as Oprah.

'Oprah? Right, and how are you going to dress up as Oprah? You don't exactly look like her.'

Don't be racist.

'I'm not being racist, Zee. Oprah Winfrey is black and you are not.'

This is what racism must feel like …

'Fuck, Zee, we're not having this discussion,' I go back into the changeroom to return to my civvies clothes.

I knew I should have made you watch The Eye *documentary with me*, she calls out from her cubicle. *But I forgive you.*

'It's called *Blue Eye, Brown Eye* idiot, and you're the one who hasn't seen it. I told you about it, remember? And I don't need your forgiveness.'

My people have a long memory.

'What people? You don't *have* people. Fine, you go as your hero, Oprah. And I'll go as my hero, Sylvia Plath, but I'm still not having a party.'

Sylvia Plath stuck her head in an oven.

'Whatever. I'm not having a party.'

Fine, says Zoë, in a pissed off five-year-old way. *Hey, you know Shaun says he's going to turn up tonight and hotslice us when we're not looking.*

'I can't believe you think it's reasonable putting your hands between someone's thighs. It's disgusting.'

I know, she grins. *Shaun hotsliced me last week when I was serving a customer. I screamed. It's a total violation — which is, of course, why we do it to each other. Anyway, he's threatening to come to the RE tonight and get us. So keep your eyes peeled and your bottom clenched. Sharon obviously didn't mind you taking today off to get these costumes?*

'No, no, she insisted. She still has to work late this week so I think Alex has gone into After-School care this afternoon. Now, we'd better hire these and head home. Otherwise we won't make it to the RE and the manager is expecting us to start collecting at seven pm.'

33

The RE is packed. And the appearance of Ms Budd and myself dressed as nuns with Red Cross donation tins just succeeds in pumping up the atmosphere. We go to the bar and after getting pinched on the bum, I decide that we need to have a warm-up drink or two to get ourselves psychologically ready for asking people for donations. As I lick the last drop of scotch out of my glass, Zoë stubs out her cigarette and says *Righto* and the both of us know that it's time to get started. We check in with the RE Manager and get the all-clear and then it's time to head out.

We decide early on to stick together, so we "Excuse me", "Hi how are you all?", "We were wondering …" our way through the crowd. It surprises me the number of people who actually think we're real nuns. Zee plays along with it completely and even baptises one drunk guy who claims that he ran into Jesus in the men's toilets a few minutes earlier. As the night wears on Zoë blesses everyone who gives us money. I can't help but think she would be the best thing to happen to the Christian Television Association since *Sing Me A Rainbow*.

Two hours later and we're sitting in the Sportsman's Bar counting our collections. In our donation buckets we have collected $262.85, two soggy bar coasters (courtesy of two UQ rugby boys), a Stoli bottle top, a Kindersurprise toy (present from the baptisee) and six cigarette butts (Zoë).

'It's nowhere near enough.'

You're not meant to be in this anyway. Right?

'I know. But I'd like to think that I could at least raise the $500 entry fee.'

And then Pat Benatar comes on the juke box and I begin to sink into another depression. Zoë rolls her eyes and says, *Let's go back out and start asking people for their confessions,* but I shake my head and say, 'You go, I'll be out there soon.'

I'm going to see if I can find Shaun and hotslice him before he hotslices us.

I sit and drink. More than I should. My wimple is itching me. I keep drinking. Each sip of alcohol makes me feel warm and fuzzy. It slowly makes me feel like all the shit that's happening in my life doesn't matter. I can get through all of this. And still be a winner. In control. A penguin with a plan.

I push aside my three empty Stoli bottles and decide to find Zoë. My legs are a bit wobbly but I push my way through the sardine crowd looking for a fellow sister. And that's when I see her playing pool. She's leaning over the table, cigarette teetering on her lips, lining up a corner shot. Her habit is blowing slightly in the breeze. *Six ball. Side pocket*, she mutters. And like everything in Zoë's life, the shot goes according to plan.

I clap wildly. She looks up.

Hill, you're pissed.

'Nah, I'm alright,' I say, getting comfortable.

Yeah? Well could you maybe wait until after this games finished to lie down on the felt? You're moving the balls.

'I'm married,' I say, getting up and deciding instead to sit cross-legged on the ground.

Yeah, well Troy's a dick.

'To God', I call up to her. 'I'm married to God.'

Well, I hope this time you asked for a pre-nup! Zoë laughs, as if she's been very funny.

'So, what you're saying is that I'm difficult to live with. Even God would want to divorce me. Even God would serve me with papers and claim irreconcilable differences.'

Yeah, but you could hit him with bigamy. He's married to me too, remember?

'Not even God's faithful. Men, they're all the same.'

Nah, not all men are bastards. Some of them are dead. Eight ball, corner pocket.

I watch Zoë's legs lean over the table and hear the click of the black doing what it's told. *Gentleman, that'll be eighty bucks. Thanks for playing.* She squashes the notes into her back pocket. *Hey,* she says, nodding in the distance. *Look who's here.*

I tip my head backwards and see the back of a familiar — though upside-down — head. Shaun. Shaun the hotslicer.

Ha ha, I whisper to myself. I'm going to get him. It's hotslice time.

I slowly get to my feet, fantasising how great this revenge is going to be. I'll sneak up behind him, I'll line my hand up with his upper thigh area, I'll slip the hand in and shock the shit out of him! Shaun will turn, horrified. And I am victorious again. Rachel Hill is back on top. As I weave my way through the crowd, I see his head in the distance. I creep up behind him. I line up my right hand and then with lightening speed I whip my hand in and out between his legs.

Shaun's head spins round.

Except tonight, Shaun has Dave Howard's face. Weird. He is horrified, though. And that's when two RE bouncers are upon me, dragging me outside. And it occurs to me that ...

(a) Dave Howard and Shaun look very similar from the back.

(b) I have just hotsliced Dave Howard.

As the bouncers drag me out to the carpark, a scene is created. Possibly because I am kicking and screaming as they pull me along.

Someone yells out, *They're 86-ing the nun* and someone else says, *The nun just felt up Dave Howard.*

Once outside, the cold air acts as a natural sobering tonic while the bouncers give me the, *You're banned from here. That type of behaviour is not tolerated* speech away from the crowds and where my hands can do the least amount of damage to other people's nether regions.

What the hell just happened? Zoë appears.

I start to cry.

Rach?

'I thought it was Shaun.'

Who?

'The guy you pointed out. I thought it was Shaun.'

It was Dave Howard!

'Well, I know that NOW. I just put my hand between his thighs.' I wipe my runny nose on the sleeve of my habit.

You hotsliced Dave Howard? Zoë starts to laugh. *You are such a Creeping Jesus!*

'It's not funny.'

We both sit in silence.

'I feel so dirty.'

Would Rachel Hill and Zoë Budd please come to the RE Manager's Office, says someone over the loud-speaker.

'I think we're about to get told off. I think the manager is going to ban us from the RE.'

No, he won't know. Just act cool. He's probably just going to ask us how the collection went.

The bouncers nod grudgingly when I tell them that my name has been called and that I have to go back inside to see Steve.

Head down, I follow Zoë into Steve's office and the cruel fluoro lights make me feel nauseous.

Just wait here, says one of the bar staff.

Hey, I meant to tell you that I won us an extra hundred bucks on the pool game.

'Tell me you weren't gambling with our donations…'

Let's remember which one of us just put their hands between some guy's legs.

I keep my head down and stare at my feet. Not even looking up when the office door opens. Zoë can do the speaking. She'll get us out of this.

I think you dropped this.

I recognise that voice. I look up. Dave Howard is standing in front of me holding out my Red Cross donation tin.

Shit.

It's Rachel Hill, isn't it? Rachel Hill, I'm like the Pied Piper? Rachel Hill, I've got scurvy? Rachel Hill, I write porn?

Actually, it's erotic fiction, and it was mine, pipes up Zoë. *What did you think of it?*

Well, I didn't read the whole thing, says Dave Howard, a little perplexed.

Fine, says Zoë, pissed off.

What?

'I thought you were somebody else.'

Dave Howard faces me again.

'I am so sorry. I just, I thought you were Zoë's boss Shaun and he was threatening to hotslice us tonight when we weren't looking. And I was looking at you upside down and I've had a bit to drunk. Drink. I'd had a bit to drink. And I knew that I recognised the back of your head but I just thought it was Shaun. Not you. And the porn thing was an accident. Honestly.'

Well, I think …

'This is just such a mess. This isn't what was meant to happen. My whole life is just one big bloody mess. I'm married and my parents don't know, I'm entered in a Miss Brisbane pageant that clearly I won't win because I can't even raise the $500 entry fee.'

And she's married, points out Zee.

'Thank you, Zoë. My former colleagues think I want to sleep with *Sesame Street* cast members and now I have embarrassed myself in front of Dave Howard, my favourite author, three times no less. I meant to hotslice Shaun, really. I'm not a Creeping Jesus. I'm NOT.'

Okay, okay. And he says it slowly, both times, as though he really means it. Or means something. *There's a lot going on, clearly. And I'm not even going to ask about the Creeping Jesus thing. But, Rachel — what the fuck is a hotslice?*

And so I go through the degradation of explaining the physical act, the creeping up behind the intended victim, the zeroing in on the thigh-high target and then the lightening fast movement where you do indeed whip your hand between their legs somewhere between knee and crotch. Suddenly, hotslicing seems a lot less hilarious than usual and somewhat more like an assault.

And this is a thing? This is a thing you actually do to people? What are you? A rugby league player?

Zoë laughs out loud and so do the two RE bar staff who I have just realised are sitting in the office counting change and filling out forms. I can feel myself going magenta red.

So what's the next step? You turn up in public places dressed like a nun, allegedly collecting for charity, and yet you're only there to put your hand between people's legs. And that's not really nice.

He's got a point, says Zoë.

But, I can see you're going through a hard time. But I think maybe it'd be good if you had someone to talk to. Maybe someone objective, outside the situation. Just to talk things through with. Maybe even someone professional. That kind of thing's fine, right? Particularly for complicated situations. And then, if you can sort out a few of your issues and we happen to bump into each other down here again, everything can be okay between us. Can't it?

'What do you mean "talk to someone"? You think I'm mental, don't you? I'm not mental. I used to be a Features Editor for a magazine. I shop with a fucking map.'

And he says, *Nobody's saying that shopping with a map isn't a very organised thing to do.*

'Now I know how Sylvia Plath felt. My life is just like *The Bell Jar*. I'm surrounded by unnecessary chaos.'

Have you read The Bell Jar*?*

'Well, not exactly.'

Not exactly?

'Not at all. But I had to answer a question about her in Trivial Pursuit once.'

Well, that's practically the same thing. I'm sure she'd find that very rewarding. Perhaps you should get some help if you think you've got anything in common with Sylvia Plath. Things didn't work out too well for her.

She stuck her head in the oven, says Zoë, nodding wisely.

Anyway, Steve said he was happy for me to handle this. So let's just forget it ever happened. Okay? See you around, Rachel Hill. And with that he walks out of the office.

As Zoë and I make our way back out to the carpark, Zoë asks if I want to head into the Casino or into some clubs in the Valley.

'Nah,' I say. 'But you go. And you can take my car if you'll drop me home first.'

When I get home I head straight to the kitchen for a glass of water, ignoring the seductively bright light of the oven timer. I climb into bed in my habit and fall asleep.

34

I'm running late for Alex on Friday morning. My hair looks smashed and an icepick is rattling around in my head. I try to call the Moore's to let Sharon know that I'm on my way but the phone line is engaged. Then I remember that Zoë still has the Mazda, so I grab the keys to Patricia's VW Golf.

I pull up to the Moore's house and run up the driveway, still in the process of shoving shoes on my feet with a piece of Vegemite toast in my mouth, willing my hair into behaving like a responsible adult. Alex is standing on the front doorstep in her nightie, hands on hips, when I approach. My mouth and mind are on short spin.

'Hey Alex, sorry I'm late, sorry I'm late.' I look at my watch. Oh God, it's 7.30 already. 'Come on, we have to get you into your uniform.' I lick the crumbs off the corner of my vegemite-stained mouth. 'Where's Mum? Sharon?' I call out. 'Sharon? Sorry I'm late. Where's Mum, Alex?' I say, walking past her.

In the kitchen, she whispers, not moving.

'Come on. Come on, we got to get moving this morning.' I turn around when I realise that Alex is failing to follow me into the house.

She stands and stares at me.

'Come on, Alex,' I say. 'Come into the house. We're going to be late for school.'

She looks me in the eye and says, *Snowy's dead*.

Sharon mouths *Hi* when I walk into the kitchen. She's on the phone to someone, writing down notes, making a lot of 'uha' noises. I turn to see where Alex has gone but she has disappeared.

Sharon puts the phone down.

Hi. How did last night go?

'Fine. Good. Look, sorry I'm late. I just ...'

Sharon waves her hand in the air as if to vanquish my wrongdoings.

'So, Alex said that Snowy died. Is that ...'

Oh God, Rachel, it has just been the strangest morning. I woke up to find Alex pushing Snowy along in her pram out in the backyard. I didn't think anything about it until Alex kept saying that Snowy was having a big sleep-in. She thought he was just sleeping. I glanced inside the pram and, I mean, I could see straight away that he wasn't. He wasn't sleeping. Poor thing.

'Was he sick or …?'

No, no, I mean, he must have been sixteen. I think he just passed away during the night. Old age. I knew it would happen eventually. I just …

Sharon starts to cry.

'I'm so sorry. Are you okay? Here, sit down.'

I got him as an 18th birthday present from my parents. God, stupid crying over a cat, isn't it. It's just that it's been the three of us since Alex was born. He was one of the family. That's all. She does a half-laugh and rubs her eyes. *The stupid thing is that Alex is coping better than me. God, you must think we're mad.*

'No, no, of course not. I know what it's like to lose a pet. They're like people with fur. No, I mean, I'm just so sad to hear that he died. So how is Alex really coping with it? She seemed a bit stunned when I saw her at the door before.'

You know, I've sat down with her and explained it to her but I'm not sure she really gets it. Or wants to get it. She's going to be so lonely now. Snowy was like her play-mate. She sighs heavily and smooths down her hair. *Look, I've got to get going. I'm going to be late for work.*

Alex? I've got to go to work now. Okay? Alex? Sharon calls out but there's no answer. *I think she's out the back playing. I called the vet first thing this morning and thankfully Dr Munroe came and took Snowy away — so at least we don't have to deal with that. The whole pet burial thing in the backyard.*

She takes a final swig of her now-cold coffee and hands me the mug as she heads for the door.

No point getting upset. These things happen. Alex has to learn about death and loss like everyone else.

'But it's always hard when you're little, isn't it?'

Well she's got me. She ruffles through her bag for tissues before walking out the front door.

With Sharon gone, I go on an Alex-hunt. It doesn't last long. I find her sitting on her swing in the backyard. A crumpled little figure with wild knotty hair and grubby bare feet, glaring out at the sun, as if it has betrayed her simply by rising today.

'Hey,' I say.

She doesn't answer me. Instead, I watch her small body push forward in an attempt to swing higher. Faster. Further away from this conversation.

'Want to come inside and have some breakfast with me?' I ask, sitting down on the swing beside hers.

She doesn't answer.

'It's good fun swinging, isn't it?' I say, pushing myself off the ground and into the morning.

When's Snowy coming back? she demands, looking straight ahead, concentrating hard on keeping herself high.

'Well. Snowy's not coming back, is he? Snowy died this morning, didn't he?' I say, rocking back and forth.

We swing some more.

So, will Snowy be home when I get back from school?

'Well no, no I don't think he will, will he? Because he's gone to be an angel in cat heaven. Because he was very old, wasn't he?'

Her legs instantly go tense, sticking out straight in front of her in an effort to make herself go faster.

'Remember when you tried to make him eat jelly last week? Wasn't that funny?'

But the vision of Snowy with red jelly on his nose is no longer funny. I should know that. And so, Alex doesn't answer me. She just swings harder. Higher.

I don't want to go to school. Her voice floats down from the adjacent monkey-bars.

My instinct is to say, 'Well, Alex, you have to go to school.' But I don't. And for once I think about the reasons why she might not want to be at school today, surrounded by her friends, all of whose pets woke up fine and healthy this morning. Unlike her. Surrounded by people who haven't been touched by death at 7.35 this morning.

'Okay,' I say. 'Okay. No school. If it's okay with your mum, you can spend the day with me.'

And Snowy? she looks at me hopefully.

I smile at her sadly and say, 'Let's start by having pancakes for breakfast.'

35

While Alex tucks into her pancakes, I ring Sharon and check that it's okay that Alex misses a day of school. Sharon gives us the thumbs up, but reminds me that I must let the school know that Alex won't be in. I decide to ring the office, but then Alex says that her reading book is due back in to Mrs Healy and that she'll get in huge trouble if it doesn't get handed in today. So rather than ring, I decide that we'll swing by just before nine am, we'll hand in the book and I'll tell Alex's teacher myself that Alex will be with me for the rest of the day.

Alex decides that she would like to wear her ballet tutu. The huge tulle skirt is sitting on top of her dollhouse but the leotard is in the washing basket. And even though I know that it has a big stain down the front and that it's far from appropriate, I let her wear it. Because I can remember what it's like to want to wear a tutu all day. And really, there's never a wrong time to wear pink tulle.

In the car Alex doesn't say much. Her stiff tulle skirt fights the constraints of the seatbelt. Awkward and uncomfortable like its owner. I park in front of the gates and the nervous ballerina follows behind me cautiously as we walk up to her classroom. Her classmates are already inside causing mild six-year-old-style anarchy with Clag, pipe cleaners and felt. Mrs Healy is saying something about tuckshop bags and *Rowan, please don't cut India's hair* and *Hands up, who ordered milk this term?* Alex decides to wait outside when I go up to Mrs Healy's desk. A woman in her early fifties, I'd guess, with short dark hair that looks as if it's living out the retirement years of a bad perm and an ample bosom taunting the buttons on her polyester blouse. She's reading a manual and doesn't look up, despite the fact that I'm standing right in front of her desk.

'Excuse me? Mrs Healy?'

Yes? She looks up from her reading, peering over her glasses.

'I'm Rachel Hill. Alex Moore's nanny.'

What can I help you with, Miss Hill? She takes off her glasses and puts down her manual in a deliberate way, as if to indicate that I have her full attention. And this interruption had better be good.

'Well, I just wanted you to know that Alex's cat, Snowy, died this morning, so she's going to have the day off school with me.'

Mrs Healy stares up at me with a detached expression. No "sorry to hear that", no "poor little thing" – Mrs Healy just stares at me with a "We are not amused" type of expression. Clearly a graduate of the Princess Anne School of PR.

'She's depressed as you can imagine, so, yeah, I just wanted to let you know. And Alex was terrified that she'd get in trouble if she didn't hand her reading book in.'

I laugh. I laugh alone. This woman is frightening me.

'I think it was due back today. So, here it is.' I hand over *Meg and Mog*.

We really don't like the kids missing too much school and I'm sure you can understand that if all of the children took a day off every time one of their pets died, they'd never get through Grade Two.

'No, no of course not. But …'

And Alex really isn't one of the children who can afford to get behind, Miss Hill.

There's something about the way Mrs Healy says this that bugs me.

'Is Alex having trouble in class? Are you saying that she's not doing very well?'

Look Miss Hill, this really isn't something I can discuss with you. Perhaps if Mrs Moore …

'It's MS Moore.'

Perhaps if MS Moore could find the time this year to come and talk to me about Alex, I'll discuss it with her then. And she puts her glasses back on and picks up the manual in front of her and resumes reading. My audience with Her Royal Highness is clearly over.

I'm about to turn to leave but something inside me thinks 'fuck it'. I hate the way this woman is talking about Alex.

'Mrs Healy?'

She looks up. This time with an annoyed expression.

'Alex is an incredibly bright, intelligent little girl. She just needs to be inspired. That's all. When I'm with her she is brimming with questions and ideas for projects. I've looked after a lot of kids in my time and Alex is probably one of the brightest kids I've been in contact with. I'm just sorry that your teaching style doesn't inspire her. But I will be sure to mention this discussion with Alex's mother. No doubt she will be in contact with you very soon. Now I'd better let you go, I can see that you're busy …'

I nod towards her reading manual.

'But you might want to stop that child over there from eating his entire tub of Clag.'

As I turn to leave I see Alex standing in the doorway staring at Mrs Healy and myself.

'Come on, champ,' I say. 'Let's go home.'

Alex smiles up at me with what looks like gratitude and grabs my hand tightly as we walk back to the car.

The 15-minute drive home from school is a good one. We sing along to Britney Spears punctuated by debates ranging from whether we think Brianna, a girl in Alex's class, is telling the truth when she says she is an alien (we're undecided and are awaiting further evidence), to whether Cleopatra was the lady who got killed in a car accident in Paris because she wasn't wearing a seatbelt (we think not likely). We finish with a discussion on how many leaves there might be on trees (we decide that there would be at least a hundred but maybe not quite five thousand infinity), with me opting to explain the concept of infinity another time.

But when we get home Alex sees Snowy's empty pram sitting in the garage.

Snowy's dead, she says matter-of-factly.

'Yes,' I say.

I miss him, she says.

'Me too.'

I suggest that we make a memorial to Snowy in the backyard. Alex draws a picture of her and Snowy skipping and I make a small cross out of some paddlepop sticks and write Snowy's name on it.

We bury Snowy's favourite toy, a woollen mouse, in the backyard under a tree and stick the cross in the ground. I say a little prayer while Alex sings the *Cat-Dog* cartoon theme song – which she insists was Snowy's favourite. We reminisce about the time that Snowy vomited on Sharon's knitting and what a good skipper he was and how much he loved watching cartoons and wearing glitter and riding in the pram and sleeping at Alex's feet every night. We talk about how my old dog, Murphy, is up there in pet heaven and how the two of them will be best friends. Then Alex asks me if the lizard that Snowy killed last Wednesday will be up there too. In pet heaven? And wouldn't the lizard be kinda angry at Snowy for biting off his head? I tell her that everyone is friends in pet heaven and that the lizard will have a new head now and hence forgotten all about the decapitation incident.

And then Alex begins to cry. She sobs big fat shiny tears and I don't try to stop her or tell her that she shouldn't be sad. Because she should. She is a little girl who has lost her best friend. So I hold her on my lap and let her cry for Snowy, while I stroke her hair. Once the tears have dried up, I say 'Maybe sometime soon, you and Mummy can go to the shop and find a new kitten? And you can teach it how to skip and tell it all about Snowy.'

Maybe, she sniffs. *But not today. Today I just want to think about Snowy.*

And I say, 'I know exactly what you mean.'

36

Friday night and I'm sitting alone with a tub of vanilla low-fat icecream in one hand and a Milo tin in the other. I have developed a system of taking a scoop of icecream, dipping it into the Milo and then shovelling it into my mouth. I go into Mum and Dad's bedroom and survey myself in front of the full-length mirror. I have nice eyes. And good hair – nice and thick like Patricia's. And my ears are pretty good, as far as ears go. My mouth's a little small but workable. Good neck and shoulders. And then I focus on my chest. It's like two aspirins sitting on an ironing board. I reach for the Cottee's Chocolate Topping.

I watch some Friday night TV and I think about what a long time it's been since the aspirins and I have seen Matt.

Not since the Tina Turner viewing. Maybe when I fell asleep I started to dribble. Or snore. Maybe I was repulsive and he felt that he just had to get away from me. Maybe … The phone rings. Naturally I think it's destined to be Matt – the way it would be if my life were a movie. But when I pick up the phone, it's not Matt. It's Jason. Jason asking me if we're still on for Archerfield International Speedway tomorrow night, *per favore*.

I have flashbacks of the BBQ sex we had. This is not a good idea, me and Jason on a date. I need to tell him it was a mistake. That we both need to move on. And I start to tell him this. I take his heart and begin crushing it with my bare hands. Then Jason tells me that I am the most beautiful woman he has ever seen and that Angus's engagement party was the best night of his life. And how – thanks to me – he won't be turning eighteen still a virgin.

I tell him I'll pick him up at seven.

Should I bring my Hot Latin Lovers tape to play in the car? Because there's a song on it that reminds me of us.

Us? Now he's recklessly tossing around the 'sharing pronoun'? Stop using the sharing pronoun, I want to scream. There is no 'us'. There is a you. And there is a me. But at no point do him and I merge to become one word.

'Sure,' I say. 'Bring the tape.'

On Saturday evening, it takes me longer than expected to choose an outfit that won't look out of place amongst that heady mix of stone-wash denim and mullets. In the end I choose my 1989 St Peters Chicks with Sticks hockey jersey (hoping this will remind Jason of the age-chasm between us) and a pair of jeans. When I pick him up Jason's mother follows him out to the car and says, *He needs to be home by eleven. He has assignments due next week.*

The drive to Archerfield is unbearably slow. Jason tells me that he is thinking of taking Salsa lessons. I play Mike and the Mechanics in the car, telling him that I am holding out for a reunion concert. Jason casually mentions that apparently Goldie Hawn is ten years older than Kurt Russell *and they've been together forever, babe.* I tell him that I think I can see the first liver spots on my hands. Jason tells me that the great thing about older women is that they know what they want and aren't as obsessed with their appearance as girls his own age. I tell him to shut up and put his seatbelt on.

The evening is a mild disaster, as first dates with toy-boys go. It depresses me that he doesn't know who James Freud is. That he can't remember how bad Simon Le Bon's hair was in the 'View to A Kill' film clip. That he thinks Bananarama is a smoothie from Baskin & Robbins. Instead, we sit and chat about car engines and whether he really wants to be an architect and how great the new Ben Folds CD is. The high-point of the evening is a muscly blond guy making eyes at me from two rows in front and then coming up to introduce himself when I'm in line for a hotdog. The low-point of the evening is learning that the muscly blond guy's name is Susan.

By the time I drop Jason home at eleven pm we have decided to break up. Apparently Jason cares about me – very much in fact – but isn't really looking for a long-term thing right now. *I think Mum's right, you know? Women your age are on the hunt for husbands and I'm just not ready to settle down yet.*

I say nothing, watch him get out of the car and go inside. Then I throw his Hot Latin Lovers tape out the window and reverse over it.

When I pull into the driveway I see Fiona's red Laser parked out the front of Matt's place. Matt who hasn't called me or visited me for three days. I wish he would come round so that I could show him that I am ignoring him. And my fingers hurt from pressing *10# on the touchpad of the phone.

At 11.25pm I am sound asleep on the couch after watching repeats of *Little House on the Prairie*. At 11.26pm I am woken by someone knocking on the front door. Disoriented at first, I stumble into the hallway, turn on the outside light and look through the peephole.

It's Fiona.

37

As soon as I open the front door, Fiona launches into a series of rambling sentences, talking to me like we are well acquainted. I have fleeting moments of comprehension. She wants me to come over to the house. She's run out of some tablet and will have to drive to a 24-hour chemist to pick some up. Usually Matt is here to cover for her. She really wanted him to go on the end-of-exams pub-crawl with the other uni students for once. She should only be gone for a little while – twenty minutes maximum. All I have to do is sit with her.

This is the part I don't get.

'Sit with who?'

Helen. She's asleep. You won't have any problems. Just sit in the room and read some magazines. I'm so sorry to do this to you but we can't leave her alone and I didn't know who else to go to and I know how close you are to Matt …

'No, no, it's fine. I don't mind.' I turn around to go back into the house to grab my keys and then I stop and turn around. 'Fiona? I really don't think I understand what I'm doing exactly. I don't quite know what's going on.'

Well, Helen's in the middle stages of her dementia, a time when we really don't like to leave her alone in the house for too long. Just in case she wakes up and doesn't know where she is. The last time we left her for no more than twenty minutes we found her sitting in the garden of the people who live across the road. She started weeding their garden. She thought it was her house back in Melbourne. She had no idea that she was weeding someone else's lawn. If she wakes up she'll probably just think you're me and go back to sleep. Her eyesight's not great. And if she asks for Matt, just tell her that he's on his way home.

'So Matt …'

…is out. With some uni friends. Yeah. You know, I just think he deserves to have some time-off. A night out with his friends. As her primary carer, he spends so much time here looking after Helen — you've been a saving grace for him, actually. He's been so much happier in the last few weeks since he started teaching you piano.

I must have a slightly confused look on my face because then she adds, suspiciously, *But you knew all this, right? Matt told you about his mum, didn't he?*

I smile reassuringly and say, 'It's fine,' turn off the TV, grab my keys and follow her out the door — all the time trying to piece together what the hell's been going on.

★ ★

As Fiona lets herself into Matt's house I am reminded again that I have never set foot here. In the weeks that I have known Matt, we have spent every moment at my house, never his. Never here. He always made the excuse that his place was a typical uni-student disaster zone. As I walk into the hallway, it becomes obvious that it is anything *but*. The first thing that grabs my attention is the grand piano sitting in the corner of the living room – as if by being in the corner it's out of the way and hard to see. Christ. There are two over-stuffed floral print sofas and a rather expensive-looking coffee table. The walls are covered with photographs – some black and white, some colour. There are trinkets on the shelves and row upon row of hard-cover books. This is so far removed from what I was expecting. I was expecting a uni flat. I was expecting beanbags and garage-sale chairs and a coffee table made from crates and empty pizza cartons sitting near the front door. And this is not that. This is …

Rachel?

Fiona has gone ahead into what I can only guess is Mrs Harding's bedroom. I look up and she is standing outside a door, a few metres down the hallway. She is beckoning me to follow, as if I am Alice and she is the White Rabbit. Enticing me to follow, hurrying me up.

I approach the bedroom door and Fiona says, *Wait here,* and goes back into the kitchen. I do as I am told, standing at the doorway, peering into the dimly-lit bedroom. I am immediately overwhelmed by its scent. A mixture of lilac and mustiness. Old and yet affectionate. The smell of a grandmother's hug. Inside I can see no shadows of Mad Hatters or Queen of Hearts. My eyes become a camera lens, trying to focus and adjust to the light. Slowly, I see the silhouette on the wallpaper — climbing roses or vines that creep from foot to ceiling. I see an enormous bed enveloped by a snug-looking patchwork quilt. I see a rather comfy chair in the corner that seems to have a book lying on it, face down. And only then, when my eyes wander back to the bed, do I notice her amongst the ruffles and pillows. A tiny woman with long silver hair, a Clara Bow mouth and the face of an autumn leaf. A woman who is sound asleep. And she is beautiful.

There's a stack of mags there in the corner. Fiona re-enters the room, oblivious to my thoughts. She moves over to a dresser drawer and starts to fill out forms in some kind of logbook. At the same time she checks and measures different medications that sit on top of the dresser, the way some other ladies might line up their perfumes. And that's when I slot another piece of the puzzle into the jigsaw.

'You're the nurse,' I say out loud, more a statement than a question. Fiona is a nurse. Mrs Harding's nurse.

Mmm-hmm, she says, adjusting Mrs Harding's covers. There is something about Mrs Harding's blue flannel nightie, buttoned up to her chin, that makes her look like a doll. I have an overwhelming desire to touch her hair. *Matt calls me when he needs a hand — which has been a fair amount lately. I mostly do night shift to give Matt a break but I also do some day shifts — depending on what he needs. That's the thing with dementia — after a while they need round the clock care. And Matt's resisting putting Helen into a full-time nursing home situation. Although I've told him that he's going to have to eventually. It's just too big a job. And he deserves to have a life.* She stands for a moment, pushes some loose strands of hair behind her ears, then she surveys the room, hands on hips. *I might just open this window a little more.*

Okay, she says, seemingly satisfied that Helen is comfortable and in safe hands. *Here's my mobile number if you have any problems. I won't be gone longer than twenty minutes. And like I said, she probably won't wake up. If she does, then just tell her that I'll be back soon. You know …*

No, I want to say. I don't know. I want to go back to watching *Little House on the Prairie.* But suddenly Fiona is heading back towards the front door leaving me in a situation that I'm far from happy with.

If Matt gets back before me just tell him that we ran out of Exelon and that I've gone to get some made up at the Medical Centre.

'Sure I …'

And help yourself to tea, coffee, whatever. Thanks, Rachel. Be back soon. Then she stops in her tracks and turns back around to face me.

You're okay with this, right?

This is my chance to escape. To say, frankly, no it's not. I'd really like to help you but I can't.

'I'll be fine.'

Good, thanks. I'll be back before you know it. She probably won't even wake up. And remember, tea, coffee … she nods her head towards the kitchen.

'Yeah, I'll be right.'

Okay. Bye.

And now I'm standing alone in Matthew Harding's kitchen, my mind shifting like a Rubik's cube, trying to decipher what exactly I have learnt in the last half-hour. That Matthew doesn't live alone. That he lives with his mum who has dementia. That he isn't doing a thesis. No, he probably is doing a thesis — she said that he was out with uni friends. And Fiona is the nurse. Which explains why the car is there so often. So … I just … my mind is racing. So, this is Matt's life. I walk into the living room.

So *this* is Matt's life.

I look around the pristine kitchen at the matching flour jars and spaghetti canisters and the array of recipe books. This is SO not a uni flat. But then I had established that already, hadn't I? I had established that Matt has been telling me lies. This is a family home. Not a bachelor pad where he's been having sex on the kitchen counter. Matt lives with his mother. I walk into the lounge room and decide to have a closer look at the photographs hanging on the wall. There are dozens. Matt as a toddler at the beach, playing with a bucket and spade. Matt on his first day of school. Matt surrounded by other young boys with a cake that says Happy 10th Birthday Matt. Matt in a scout uniform standing in front of a bus. Matt sitting on his mother's lap at a piano. On the opposite wall there are certificates – all made out to Matthew Harding. First Prize in the Victorian Junior Piano recital. Highly Commended in some Melbourne eisteddfod. I turn my back on these plaques and walk over to the bookshelf, where I close my eyes and run my hands over the spines of the wall of books on the shelves, feeling their texture, going into a trance just for a moment. I run my hand over the arms of the couches, I pick up a cushion and smell it – perhaps thinking that it will provide another clue. To what, I'm not sure.

I have been avoiding the grand piano, as if I am playing hard to get and trying to pretend that I have failed to even notice its presence. I walk over to it. I run my fingers lightly over its top and I leave smudgy fingerprints that I could wipe away if I wanted to. But I don't. I have no real urge to sit down and play it the way that I thought I would. This piano deserves better than my messed-up version of 'Jessica's Theme'. It deserves symphonies. Mr Holland's Opus. That kind of thing. But I sit down at the seat anyway and that's when I notice the small silver frame perched on the left hand side – out of sight from where I was standing before. It is a black and white photo of a young woman. I pick it up and study it carefully. She's wearing a knee-length dress with a loose belt tied around the waist. She's sitting on the bonnet of a sports car, throwing her head back laughing at a joke that the photographer has probably told her. There are loose curls in her dark shoulder-length hair, which sits easily on her shoulders. The smile on her face reaches all the way to her eyes. I'm not sure I've ever seen a woman so joyful. And it only enhances her beauty. That's when I realise that this woman in the photograph is the woman in the bedroom. This is Matt's mother.

I put the frame down. I can't believe that he kept this from me. I thought that we were friends. Close friends. And this is big. Big. A huge deal. An important thing to share. I can't believe that all this time he has been nursing his mother. He should have told me. I could have helped him. Could have, I don't know, done something to help. I don't know whether to be angry or sympathetic. Or hurt.

Fiona? Fiona? calls out a voice from down the hall.

She's awake.

36

For a few seconds I stand. Frozen. Not quite sure what to do. My breathing stops.

Fiona? whispers the voice. A voice woven with threads of anxiety.

The next thing I know I am holding her hand and whispering to her, 'It's okay Mrs Harding. Matt will be home soon. Go back to sleep.' Her hand feels soft but sort of papery.

Her eyes look at me, frightened. *Where's Fiona? You're not Fiona.* Her grip on my hand tightens.

'No, I'm Rachel, from next door. Fiona has just gone out for a few minutes but she'll be back soon. And Matthew will be back soon too. Everything is okay.'

Rachel. You're Matthew's girlfriend.

'Well, I wouldn't really say …'

She puts a hand out to my face and cups it, pulling my face closer to her, *Yes, you do have beautiful eyes. You're the one who has been playing the piano? Yes? Matthew's been helping you? You're all he ever talks about, Rachel. Rachel, with the beautiful eyes.*

A smile creeps over my lips. Then I look back down at Mrs Harding and in her eyes I see such relief.

'Yes, Matthew has helped me so much with the piano. Now, can I get you anything? A glass of water? Are you thirsty? Fiona will be back any minute now. Really. And so will Matt.'

Would you get me some water please?

'Sure. Just a sec …'

I go back into the kitchen, opening every cupboard until I find some glasses. I find a water-jug in the fridge and head back to the room with the slightly too full glass.

'Here you go, Mrs Harding,' I say, entering the room only to find her with her legs swung over the side of the bed. Oh God, why can't she just lie down and go back to sleep. I wish Fiona was here.

What time is the car coming to collect me?

'What car, Mrs Harding?'

The car for the concert. How long have we got before it arrives?

'Umm, I don't know, Mrs Harding. I'm Rachel, remember? Matthew's girlfriend. And I just got you a glass of water? I'm not sure …'

Anthony will be so happy. Now, I can't remember. Did we say that the car was coming at six or six thirty?

I can feel my heart start to race. I don't know what to do. I don't know how to handle this.

'I don't know, Mrs Harding, but I bet Fiona will know. And Fiona is going to be home any minute now. Maybe you should have a rest before you go out. Matthew will be home soon too. Very soon. Any minute now. He wants to see you.'

She picks up a hairbrush by the side of her bed and says, *Mary, will you brush my hair for me? And don't tell me if you see any grey hairs, I don't want to know.*

She hands me the brush with a smile on her face and such trust in her eyes, as if she knows me, as if we're best friends. I don't know who she's seeing when she looks at me. And I don't know what to do.

Here, sit here. And she pats the mattress and motions for me to sit behind her on the bed. She smooths the creases out of her blue polka-dotted flannelette nightie and says, *I definitely think we chose the right dress. This really is one of my favourites.*

And so I start to brush. Ever so gently, I pull the bristles through her silver hair. The same way that I would brush Alex's hair, with care and tenderness. When I look up I realise that she's staring at me in the mirror that hangs opposite us on the wall.

'There you go,' I say. 'You have beautiful hair. You know, I think that Matthew is due home any minute now.'

I remember Fiona's mobile phone number in my pocket. I'll just call her. Tell her that Mrs Harding is awake and acting strange. That she's started calling me Mary. That she really does need to come back. That I'm not sure what to do.

Meanwhile, Mrs Harding is humming a tune. Her eyes have closed. God, now what do I do?

'Mrs Harding,' I say, tapping her shoulder. 'Why don't you have a lie down while we wait?'

Yes, she says, opening her eyes. *Yes.* She takes hold of my hand as she swings her legs back into bed. As she eases herself down, I pull up the quilt in the same way that I would tuck in Alex.

Where's Matthew? she says suddenly, her voice laced with panic.

'Well, he's on his …'

I want Matthew.

The recognition that had been in her eyes has evaporated. Moved out. In its place is fear. She doesn't recognise me.

I don't know you. Why are you here? Why are you in my home? She starts to cry. *Don't hurt me. Please don't hurt me.*

I put my hand out to comfort her but she screams, *Get away from me,* knocking my hand back with such force that I end up smacking myself in the lip with the hairbrush.

She scrambles to sit up, clutching the quilt to her chest and retreating to the furthest corner of the bed. *Get away from me!* she screams, her face contorting and going purple with rage. *Get away from me! Where's Matthew? Where's Matthew? Matthew!* she screams out. *Matthew!* Her breath is short and uneven, like someone hyperventilating.

My lip starts to throb and the taste of blood trickles into my mouth and onto my tongue.

Tears are beginning to well up in my own eyes.

'It's alright, Mrs Harding,' I say, 'I'm sorry, I'm sorry.' I back away towards the bedroom door, all the while fishing in my jeans pockets for Fiona's mobile phone number.

And then suddenly Matt is in the room. Soothing Mrs Harding, calming her down, talking her back off her emotional window ledge. *It's alright, Mum, I'm here, I'm here.*

She clutches him. *Matthew, that woman was trying to hurt me. She was trying to hurt me, Matthew. Tell her to go away. I missed you. Where were you? Don't leave me, Matthew. Don't leave me.*

I go back out to the hallway, shaking. My heart is racing. The blood in my mouth makes me want to throw up. I start to cry – out of nervousness and exhaustion.

I stand by myself. I can hear the murmur of Matthew's voice, soothing Mrs Harding's fears. Calming her down.

Calming me down also. I try to regain my breath and walk back out into the living room, taking a seat at the grand piano. The taste of blood lingers in my mouth. As if by instinct my fingers briefly flutter over my lip. As soon as the pain registers at their touch my hand returns to my lap. I don't hear the bedroom door shut or Matt's footsteps coming toward me. Into the lounge room.

Rachel? Matt's voice commands me to look up. He's standing on the other side of the room. I look at him, but Matt is not looking at me. He's looking up, to the left, then down to the floor, not making eye contact, as if he can't bring himself to look at me for fear of what he might do or say.

'Matt, I just …'

Don't. Just go home. NOW. And then he walks back down

the hallway, leaving me alone with the joyful woman in the silver frame.

39

'**H**ey! HEY! Get back here!'

Keep your voice down.

'Don't tell me to keep my voice down. Do you have any idea what I have gone through in the last hour?'

Well, that's just it. You shouldn't be here. This is nothing to do with you.

'Fiona came over and asked me to come and watch your mother because she had to rush out and get some tablets or something. And for the record, Fiona just assumed that I knew. About your mother. I have no clue what I'm doing here – no clue. Fiona's talking about dementia and telling me not to worry because your mother probably won't even wake up. Then your mother wakes up and, when I tell her my name, she says she knows who I am …'

Well I might have mentioned you a few times.

'Right, well, one minute she's talking to me and the next she's asking about when the car is coming to pick her up and she's calling me Mary and then all of a sudden she freaks out – starts panicking and screaming for you. I didn't do anything to her Matt, she just started like that.'

I know. He sighs.

'I was just trying to help. Just doing what Fiona told me.'

He bows his head towards his hands. *I'm sorry.*

'Why didn't you tell me? About your mum? I thought that we were close friends. I mean, I know I haven't known you long but we've spent so much time together. I can't believe that you've been keeping this from me.'

I know ... He reaches out and touches my arm.

I pull away. 'You're the one, you're the one who's been going on about telling each other about ourselves. That I'm the one who's uptight, who's difficult to get to know and the whole time you're lying.'

I haven't been lying to you.

'I feel like you don't trust me.'

Don't be ridiculous. Why does everything have to be about you? You're blowing this whole thing out of proportion. You know lots about me.

'You know what I realised tonight? That I've never even been here before. To your house. You've been in my place nearly every day since we met.' I turn my back on him and stare out the window into their bare back garden.

Rachel, you do know me. Okay, so I didn't tell you about my mum. Fine. I should have but don't act as if this means that you don't know who I am. I've been more open and honest with you than anyone else I've ever met. And what are you saying? That just because you haven't been in my house that it means you don't know who I am? I've been in your house a dozen times and I still hardly know you any better than the first day we met. Because you won't give an inch. So yeah, I've seen your kitchen and walked through your dining room, I've looked at photos of your parents and rummaged through your CD collection. And what difference has that made? None.

I take a deep breath.

'What do you want to know, Matt? Hmm? What do you want to know about me? I was a Prefect at school, got Honours at university, my best friend Zoë is a lesbian. I hate rockmelon, love salt-and-vinegar potato chips, I read *Wild Swans* but apparently am the only person in Australia who hasn't read *Angela's Ashes*. I bought tickets to see Take That, I like instant coffee, I hated the movie *Forrest Gump*, I've never seen a *Rocky* movie or any part of the *Godfather* trilogy. I sing when I'm in the shower, I once got so drunk at the RE that I fell down a flight of stairs, my favourite colour is yellow, I stay up every year and watch the *Eurovision Song Contest*, I tell everyone that I only have one sugar in my coffee but I actually have two. I've seen every one of Michael J Fox's movies including *Little Mickey* and I hate pickle on my cheeseburger and I'm allergic to strawberries. I prefer caramel over chocolate sundaes and you know what else? With you nursing your mum? I never would have kept something like that from you. I would *never* have not told you something as big as that. *Never.* You have just made our friendship a joke.'

And that's when Fiona breezes back into the house.

Can you believe that I had to go all the way to Coorparoo just to find a 24-hour chemist?

'I was just leaving.'

I slam the screen door behind me, anger and indignation still bubbling under my skin. I storm up the footpath, make the turn up into my driveway and then, as I slot the key in the front door, I suddenly remember. I do have a secret.

I have a *husband.*

40

I don't sleep a wink on Saturday night. I lay awake staring up at the ceiling wondering what the hell I've done. Accusing Matt of keeping secrets from me, of being less than honest. And I've got a husband. How could I forget something like that?

At six am I can't stand it any longer so I ring Zoë.

Whoever this is, go away.

'It's me. You're not going to believe what I've done.'

Rach? It's 6 …09am.

'I know, I'm sorry but I need to talk to you. I've just gotten myself into the biggest mess. Can I come round?'

I'll meet you at McDonald's Indooroopilly in half an hour. You can buy me breakfast. And then she hangs up.

At 6.45am I'm standing outside Indooroopilly McDonald's staring forlornly at the adventure playground.

So what the McFuck's going on? I turn around and there's Zee wearing dark sunglasses, her men's striped pyjamas and a dressing gown. I try to bite my tongue and not comment on her attire. But I can't help it.

'You're in your pyjamas.'

I'm here, aren't I?

'Fine.'

We go inside — Zoë shuffling across the tiled floor in her slippers — order two Big Breakfasts, extra hash browns, and I tell her the events of the last 24 hours.

Mmmm. She picks hash brown out of her teeth, *So his mum's got dementia? God … wow that's really … I mean, I'm guessing that explains the bruises and stuff.*

'Well, within five minutes of me meeting her I cut my lip, so I'm guessing yeah.'

Shit … no wonder he didn't want to tell you. He's probably, I don't know, nervous about telling people. Frankly, I think you were a bit harsh on him. I mean, how about when my mum's cousin Linda got caught shovelling the fake crab salad into her own Tupperware containers during a visit to Sizzler? I mean, it's not something Mum wanted to advertise.

'What am I going to do? Last night I went off my nut at him accusing him of being dishonest, of keeping secrets from me and I'm *married*. Oh God. I'm married.'

Yeah, I tend to forget you're technically married.

'Me too.'

So have you at least signed the divorce papers yet?

'Nearly.'

How can you nearly sign divorce papers, Hill? You either have or you haven't. First things first, sign the damn things, get the damn divorce and move on from Troy. Second, you have to tell your parents and Matt. You know you're going to have to tell Matt, right?

'I know but how? How do I tell him after what I said to him last night? Maybe I don't have to tell him. Maybe I'll just get divorced and he doesn't need to know. He'll never find out.'

And maybe you two will get together eventually ... maybe you'll fall in love and maybe you'll get engaged and maybe you'll have a meeting with the priest who's going to marry you a few weeks before the ceremony just to check some details and maybe he'll say, 'So is this the first wedding for you both?' and Matt will say, 'Yes', and you'll say, 'Well actually, there was this one time in Vegas ...'

'I'm not going to marry him. Who said anything about me marrying him?'

Don't go pretending you're not even slightly interested in him. I haven't even met him and I know that there's something between you two.

'I don't know what to do.' I slump down in my booth.

These things have a habit of coming out and it's not worth the major hurt it'll cause down the track. Tell him.

'I hate this.'

You know, despite all this shit that's happening in your life, look at you — I mean, this time two months ago all you did was live and breathe that damn magazine. You never went out on the weekends unless it was a work-related function. You never got drunk. You never shagged boys behind BBQs. I'm just saying that I think since you let the reins go a little loose, you're enjoying life a bit more, letting your ...

'Hair down.'

No, your "knickers down" but "hair down" works too.

'Okay. So I have to tell people about the marriage. My marriage. Okay, okay, so I'm gonna make a list of all the people I have to tell. Here, pass me that serviette.' I grab the eyeliner from my bag and write out the following ...

People I have to tell that I got married
Mum and Dad and Caitlin
Fergus
Matthew Harding

And then I number them from one to three.

People I have to tell that I got married
1. Mum and Dad and Caitlin
2. Fergus
3. Matthew Harding

And then I underline each of them.

<u>People I have to tell that I got married</u>
1. <u>Mum and Dad and Caitlin</u>
2. <u>Fergus</u>
3. <u>Matthew Harding</u>

And put a full stop at the end of each name.

People I have to tell that I got married.
1. <u>Mum and Dad and Caitlin.</u>
2. <u>Fergus.</u>
3. <u>Matthew Harding.</u>

Rachel? Just do it.

41

I'm in the middle of studying the wedding pages of the Sunday newspaper dressed in an old tracksuit, my wet hair plastered to my skull and an avocado mask on my face, when I hear a knock at the front door. Looking through the peephole I can see that it's Matt. I'm not about to let him see me looking like this. I open the door partly with the chain still on it.

'Yes?'

Aren't you going to let me in?

'Why should I?'

Because I've got some of your mail and I meant to give it to you yesterday.

'Well, can't you just hand it to me through the door?'

Not really. It's kinda big. He lifts up a large brown box with my name typed on an envelope on the top.

'Hang on.' I unchain the door and open it up a few centimetres. 'Don't look at me, I have an avocado mask on my face. When I open the door you have to have your eyes closed.'

What? Why?

'Do you want to come in or not?'

Okay.

I open the door and there he stands, eyes closed holding out a box.

'Thanks.'

You're welcome. So, I'm sorry about last night. I didn't sleep at all after you left. I realised how right you were and how unfair I was on you. I should never, never have kept a secret like that from you. I don't know why I did it. I think I enjoyed having someone in my life who didn't know about my mum. Who just knew me for me not as Helen Harding's "primary carer". Someone who wasn't asking me every ten minutes how my mum was and what her latest behaviours are and … you know. Look it's no excuse, I know, there's no excuse for me keeping a secret like that.

'Well, you know, I've been thinking. I think I was a little harsh on you. Let's face it, a secret never killed anybody …'

No, no, don't try and make excuses for me, Rachel. I did the wrong thing. And if you're prepared to forgive me then I promise you that I will never keep anything from you again. Honestly. You and I, no secrets. Okay?

'Well, I …' Tell him. Tell him. Tell him.

Please Rachel?

'Okay. No secrets.' Rachel Hill = Big fat liar.

And I'd really like to sit down with you and tell you about my mum. Explain a few things.

'Do you have time for a coffee now?'

Sure. But can I open my eyes?

'I suppose. But if you make one crack about how I look, you're out.'

Matt doesn't say anything about my appearance – tracksuit, wet hair and face mask. He moves around the kitchen with ease, getting out two coffee mugs, putting the kettle on, even putting out a plate of almond bread. We decide to sit outside on the veranda steps.

So, how's your lip?

'It's not too bad. Don't worry – I did it to myself, fell backwards.'

She doesn't mean to do it you know …

'Yeah, I know, Matt.'

Fiona gets it the worst. Whenever she has to convince Mum to get changed or take a shower Mum just freaks out. Fights her. Some days Fiona leaves here black and blue. She just, I don't know, becomes someone else. She sees us and thinks we're strangers. He sighs. *She just gets scared, you know, that we're trying to hurt her.* He looks up at me. *She's just frightened. And that's the cruellest thing with Alzheimer's, it takes away your personality bit by bit. She's sort of in the middle stages. At first it was, you know, okay. Not too bad. She started off forgetting little things. I used to pop round for visits once or twice a week and I started to notice it. She couldn't find her car keys. Or she'd leave the stove on. Or I'd tell her something and then she'd ask me the same question a couple of hours later. When we finally got it diagnosed I decided to move back in with her, to take care of her. But it's getting progressively worse. One time I found her sitting in the car in the garage. She was all dressed up ready to go somewhere — but she couldn't remember where it was she was meant to be going. She had no idea. That was a year ago.*

Matt starts to pick at loose threads on his khaki shorts.

Now she has times when she doesn't even recognise me.

'And who's Mary? She started calling me Mary the other night.'

That's her sister. Mary used to travel with us on the road — sort of as Mum's assistant and a babysitter for me.

'Oh.'

It's just so weird. The whole thing. She can't remember the conversations we had yesterday but she can remember every single piece of music she learnt as a child. She can remember every concert she played. Every award she's won. What dresses and evening gowns she used to own. But she can't remember if we have a cat. Or what street we live on. Or who Fiona is.

'But when she first woke up and I told her who I was, she acted like she knew about me. She even said that I was your girlfriend.'

Did she? She just says that kind of thing. She wouldn't know who you are and tomorrow, if I asked her, she won't even remember that you were ever in the house. Last week she kept thinking that Fiona was my wife. She probably just got excited because you said you were a friend of mine and you're a girl. With or without dementia all mothers want their sons to find a wife. He laughs resignedly.

'Oh.'

You seem disappointed.

'Oh no, I just … you know, I'm so sorry.'

Fiona's trying to get me to put her in the Alzheimer's Unit out at Resthaven at Brookfield. It's supposed to be excellent and Fiona says that they can give Mum round-the-clock care. She says it's only going to get worse from here on in. But I don't know. I think I'd feel like I was rejecting her, turning my back on her, you know? It just doesn't seem right.

'Well, you're obviously coping at the moment. Are you?'

Yeah, basically. There's a carer's allowance that I can claim and Fiona comes about thirty hours a week and then I can use the Day Respite Centre at Bardon — they look after her for the whole day or half a day if I want to study or go to classes or teach my neighbour the piano.

He smiles at me and gives me a friendly nudge in the arm.

But pretty soon Mum won't be able to feed herself at all. Go to the bathroom. How bad is that, when you have to wipe your own mum's arse.

We both just sit staring down at the steps, watching the ants run back and forth as they plot a plan to get to the almond bread.

I wish you'd known her before. Before she got sick. She was amazing. And you two would have gotten on so well. She was the fiercely independent type. Played in concerts all over the world. Won all types of awards. Played at the Sydney Opera House one year. I've got photos of her with Dame Joan Sutherland and Nigel Kennedy and Tim Rice. She was so strong, such an achiever. I spent so much of my childhood in her dressing room and at rehearsals, on planes travelling around the country.

'Just the two of you?'

Dad died when I was about five. Cancer. So it's been pretty much me and Mum my whole life. And that's the thing, isn't it. She's spent a lifetime looking after me, so how can I turn around and say, "This is too hard" when she needs me to return the favour?

'So, what are you going to do? As it gets worse and she needs more care, how are you going to cope?'

I try not to think about it. All I know is that while I've still got part of her here, with me, I want to make the most of it. Before she disappears completely. I'm dreading that day. The day when she looks at me and no part of her recognises who I am. And that's when I'll think about moving her into 24-hour care. Maybe.

'Well, it sounds like you have a plan then. And plans are good.'

Yeah. Plans are good, he says, staring at his mother's bedroom window that overlooks our backyard. *Let's change the topic. So, what are you up to tonight?*

'Tonight? Dunno. I still haven't done my tax. So it'll probably be a quiet night with me, the television and a calculator.'

Well, why don't you come over to my place for dinner and I'll help you with it? What are your feelings on spaghetti bolognaise and a cheap red wine accompanied by a rather dishevelled uni student?

'You've sold me.' I look at him and smile.

Once I close the front door behind Matt — promising to be round at eight pm — I suddenly remember the box that arrived. I get a pair of scissors and slice through the packing tape. Inside are twelve boxes of Froot Loops with a note that reads 'With compliments from Kellogg's Australia'.

42

On my way over to Matt's I decide that I'm not going to tell him about the marriage. There's no need. He's got enough to deal with at the moment. And it's hardly a big deal. People get married and divorced all the time. I'll just sign and send off the divorce papers tonight and then nobody else needs to know. Except Mum and Dad. And Fergus. But, apart from them, it's really no-one else's business.

You don't have to do that, you know? Matt calls out to me from the lounge room, having just checked that his Mum was still sound asleep. I continue to rinse our plates and search for the sink's plug in order to start the washing up.

'Oh I know, I want to do it. I have one rule when other people cook for me. I either have to do the washing up or try and send them to the Taringa Medical Centre. Is she okay?'

Yeah, sorry, I know I've checked on her a lot this evening but I just worry. This is what it must be like to be a parent, I guess.

'I'm nearly finished, anyway.'

Well at least let me dry.

As I hand Matt the tea-towel I notice a splodge of spaghetti sauce on his chin. I say, 'God, you're a mess', wipe my wet hands on my jeans and reach out to wipe the sauce off, the type of thing I would have done if I were with Troy. But this isn't Troy. And it's not until my fingertips are brushing Matt's chin that I realise what I'm doing. How this feels. Just the warmth of his skin, the bristly stubble that I can feel under my fingers, makes my heart beat faster.

How desperate am I? I'm getting excited wiping someone's face. I quickly withdraw my hand and say, 'All gone,' letting slip a nervous laugh.

Thanks, he says slowly, a half-smile on his lips that makes him look far too sexy for someone who has just been walking around with food on his face. I feel like he can read my mind and my face starts to heat up.

I s'pose I should return the favour.

'Wha …'

He steps closer into me, so that I can feel his breath on my face. See his chest rise and fall. I try to think unsexy thoughts. My late grandmother sipping soup through her teeth. Alex's ant painting. The theme song to *Gilligan's Island*.

You've got a little sauce on your mouth.

Just sit right back and you'll hear a tale, the tale of a fateful trip, it started on this tropic shore aboard this tiny ship ...

With his thumb Matt wipes the edge of my mouth.

... the mate was a mighty sailor's man, the skipper brave and sure ... God, he wears nice aftershave. I've stopped breathing altogether. Matt is looking me directly in the eyes.

Can I tell you something, Rachel?

'Yes,' I squeak, my voice changing pitch like a nervous twelve-year-old boy.

Since we said we'd always be honest with each other.

I swallow so loudly it practically reverberates around the kitchen.

He leans forward, putting his mouth to my ear and whispering, *You never actually had anything on your face.*

I ...

I ...

I have a husband, my mind screams to me. Pull yourself together, you slapper.

So, he says, straightening back up, *we should be doing your tax.*

What? His voice breaks through my thoughts. Wait on a second. I'm the one who's supposed to pull away. Make the excuse. Play hard to get. Stop us from going the snog, playing tonsil hockey, pash. Dammit.

Now of course I want to kiss him desperately. The bastard.

He laughs, as if he's just won the latest battle of wills and heads over to the kitchen table. *Let's get started, shall we?*

I have to tell him. If I want us to be on an even keel, I

have to tell him about Troy and the whole 'I did' incident. It's now or never.

'Matthew, I have to tell you something ...'

Hill! he says flipping through my tax return. *I've already spotted one mistake. You've ticked the box that says you're married.*

43

Uh-oh.

Look, see where it says "Did you have a spouse – married or de facto – during the last financial year"? You've accidentally ticked the "yes" box.

I just stare at Matt. Speechless. Not quite sure how to handle this.

I know what's going on here ...

Oh shit.

You're trying to stall. Look, this kind of thing isn't that hard – we'll be finished in no time. So sit down and hand me the liquid paper. And I watch, stunned, as Matt liquid papers away my marriage. In one simple stroke I've gone from a YES to a NO. An 'I did' to an 'I didn't'. No US courts involved.

When I get home on Sunday night, I rip open the plastic

of another un-used tax-pack and start all over again. Doing the real one. Copying out the same figures and outcomes but this time ticking the YES box and carefully writing the name Troy Shepard as the name of my husband. And it's time that I fixed that.

I go to the fridge and take the divorce papers out of the dairy compartment. I take them up to my bedroom and lie on my single bed, reading over them for a final time. The marriage took place on February 24 and was registered in the City of Las Vegas, County of Clark and the State of Nevada. Thereafter the parties resided together until on or about February 26. No children were born to the parties. No children were adopted by the parties. The wife is not now pregnant. As a result of irreconcilable differences that have arisen between them, the parties have lived separately and apart from one another continuously for a period of six months.

I sign my name on the remaining section.

And don't feel that much better.

And I begin to suspect that it's not the divorce that's upsetting me here. It's the fact that I'm not living the life that I thought was being sold to me when I was that seventeen-year-old over-achiever. When they pinned on that Prefect badge. The "your life is going to be full of golden moments like this" package.

When I was in Year Twelve I was told by everyone that I was going to be one of society's big achievers. That I was the type of girl who would make a difference. Be something. And I believed them. I thought that's how it was going to be. I thought that it was a given, that it was pre-determined I would have an amazing life. This type of thing wasn't meant to happen to ME. This — this life that I've got now — was meant to happen to one of those other people. Those people who never knew what they wanted to do with their lives. The ones who got bad grades and wagged class and went to parties and were always in detention.

Every time I won an award or notched up some great achievement I thought I was securing my place at the top of the line. Where the amazing people are. I was told I could do anything. Be anyone. Have it all. But now that I'm here, loitering around the finishing line, I wish someone had defined exactly what "all" was. A big salary? A good-looking spouse? A baby? Why does the definition of "having it all" revolve around things you acquire, rather than the way you feel about yourself?

Vegas isn't my problem.

It's what I thought it was going to bring me. Like the last coloured wedge in Trivial Pursuit, I thought that marriage was the one piece I didn't have and that once I slotted it in with the others, had the box set, the champagne would pop and the bells would ring and happiness would arrive in the mail alongside my credit card bill.

But it doesn't work that way. And in that scenario, there's no mention of the joy to be found in eating cupcakes with a six-year-old. Or tending to a garden and coaxing an orchid into bloom. Or writing truly bad erotic fiction that you think is a masterpiece.

I begin to think about Lisa Armstrong. I can't help but

think that if we had just seen each other, bumped into one another at Myer, then maybe we could have sat down and swapped horror stories and had a laugh and said "life can be shitty, but we'll manage". Maybe if she had just known that, that there was someone else out there whose life was far from perfect. If she ...

We wouldn't have. If we had run into each other, we would have smiled and swapped notes about where we were working and promised to ring each other soon to have coffee. Both of us knowing that it would never actually happen. We would have kept our problems to ourselves.

People say that perfection doesn't exist. But it does. And achieving a perfect-looking life isn't that hard. Perfection breezes in on a whim for all of us and stays for a few hours, a day or two. Those moments when everything is just *right*. Perfect. The problem is that we convince ourselves that we can only be happy when perfection is around. And when it does show up, we expect it to stay. Unpack. Put up its feet and make itself at home. But it can't. Never does. And instead perfection drifts out when we are unpacking the groceries. Or reading the paper. And we haven't noticed that it's gone, until it's too late. Because it leaves no forwarding address, no tell-tale clues. Just the expectation that it will return. So we wait. Wait for perfection to call and let us know when it will be back. In the meantime, we move the pictures and rugs around, covering up those foundational cracks when they begin to appear. And they always appear. Eventually.

Suddenly I feel like talking to my mum.

Caitlin's answering machine clicks on ...

Hiya, this is Caitlin. Can't talk to you right now, so leave me a message and if you're lucky I'll return it.

She always has such stupid messages.

'Mum and Dad, it's me. Just ringing to say that I hope the trip is going well and, umm, I hope the weather is still warm and ah, well, I married Troy when we went to Vegas. And now I'm going to divorce him. So yeah, give me a call back.'

44

'Alex, stop playing with your eyes, they'll fall off.'

She squirms around and scratches her sides.

It's itchy.

'I know.' I finish pulling up the zip at the back. 'Are you getting excited? Only four days to go!'

Yeah. But Julie Mooney always forgets when we're supposed to hop over to talk to the butterfly and keeps tapping me on the shoulder and asking me what happens next.

'Well, she's probably nervous, Alex. Be nice to her. Not everyone can be as good at ballet as you,' I say, and give her a poke in the tummy. 'Rehearsal starts in about five minutes so you'd better go up to the stage now. I'm going to have a look around the shops and I'll come back in an hour to take you home. Okay?'

She starts squirming again and says, *This is scratchy.* And one of her grasshopper eyes falls over her face. I fix it.

Rachel, can't you watch me for a few minutes?

'Okay, but you know I'm coming on Saturday to watch you.'

And Matt? Matt promised he would come.

'And Matt.'

She starts wriggling around. *I hate this stuff.* She pulls at the material on her stomach. *It makes me scratchy.*

'I know, but try not to think about it. Try to think about what a beautiful grasshopper you are.'

Snowy used to eat grasshoppers.

'Oh … well.'

Sometimes he would walk past with one of their legs hanging out of his mouth.

'Right, okay, well you know – you're a very friendly grasshopper who lives in a place where there are no cats to eat you.'

And then he'd vomit them up in Mum's bedroom.

'You are so disgusting!' and I pick her up and tickle her until she is doing big delicious belly laughs and her eyes are twinkling with delight.

When I get home on Monday evening I find two messages on my answering machine. The first message is from Anne Sneddon. ANNE SNEDDON. She says that she has been talking to Patricia about my "current situation". She says she wants me to call her back. I cringe at the thought of Patricia begging Anne to give me some pageant tips. I decide to ignore it. The second message is from Fergus. Gushing.

Rachel Hill, you've made it! You've just scraped through but you've managed to raise the preliminary $500. So now you get to come along tomorrow night and we'll announce which entrants will be running for each district. I think the Corinda District is between you and one other entrant – so whichever one of you raised the most will be the one who gets to proceed to compete for the Miss Brisbane title. Anyway, give me a call if you have any questions and otherwise, just come along to the Carlton Crest tomorrow night. Seven pm.

How the hell did that happen? I only sent them in $300. How could I have qualified for this? This was not the plan. There was no qualifying in the plan. Clearly, I have to tell Fergus. Obviously, I am praying to God that my unknown competitor has raised more than me and thus I am released from the shackles of this competition without having to do anything. No yucky conversations with Fergus. I've never in my life wanted to lose so badly.

I go online and check my Commonwealth Bank account. I have $97.35. In the old days I had an account balance with commas.

I eat some Froot Loops.

I wonder why Patricia hasn't called back yet.

I open a new packet of Froot Loops, sit down and play the piano. I don't even need to look at the music. 'Jessica's Theme' just flows through me and I play it the way it has always asked to be played. Conveying the uncertainty, the frustration, the persistence, the exhaustion. I think how fitting it is that this piece is called 'Breaking in the Colt,' from the scene in the movie where Jessica Harrison is putting all her passion into helping Jim Craig tame the wild horse. I wonder what they both thought it was going to bring them. Trying to tame that horse the way I have tried to tame this piece of music. And I remember what Matt said to me during our first lesson: that if I tried to control the music, it would never sound the way I wanted it to – even if I did know every note off by heart. I had to let the piece be itself, try to understand it in order to play it.

That's when it occurs to me that I just played 'Jessica's Theme' off by heart without making a single error. But the satisfaction that I thought this would bring me is missing.

I go to the veranda and call out to Matt.

You rang?

'Whatcha up to?'

Fiona's taken Mum out for a drive, so I'm just trying to do some of my thesis.

'Oh.'

What are you doing?

'Oh you know, stuff. Just hanging out.'

You're bored, aren't you?

'Maybe. Do you want to come over for dinner? I'll cook.'

As tempting as that is, I've really got to get some work done.

'I'll give you a hint for the *Mork and Mindy* theme song.'

I'll be over in ten minutes.

As soon as Matt walks in he jumps up on the kitchen bench and helps himself to the almond bread jar.

So, hit me with the hint.

'Okay, the clue is, there are no words, it's purely instrumental.'

And?

'What? That's it.'

That's it?

'Yeah – '

That's not a hint.

'Yes, it is.'

I thought you were going to sing the first line.

'No way, that's totally going to give it away.'

You interrupted my thesis for that? Tell me!

'No.'

Tell me.

'No way. Nup. You have to remember it. And you know what, this proves that I am in fact the champion of TV theme tunes. You're just an amateur.'

You know I only like you because of your almond bread.

'Yeah, yeah, that's what all the boys say.'

He laughs and jumps down off the counter. *Rachel,* he says, taking my hands in his. *There's something I've been wanting to do for a while …*

'Hey, I've got a present for you. From Alex. Wait here and I'll get it.'

I untangle myself from Matt and walk outside to my Mazda. I'm shaking. I dig around the backseat for Alex's painting of some dancing ants. I hear the distant sound of my phone ringing. Matt's going to kiss me. I haven't brushed my teeth. Okay. Okay. Somewhere here there's some chewy.

The phone's ringing. Want me to get it? Matt yells out.

'Nah – answering machine is on.'

A-ha, I find Alex's picture under some magazines on the backseat. I search for some gum but there is none. Shit. I start to walk back inside only to hear the answering machine clicking on. A familiar voice begins.

Rachel, it's your mother.

I really need to brush my teeth. Or eat an apple. I can't kiss someone unless I have fresh breath. Or I'm pissed behind a BBQ and I get to scare the shit out of their mother. Oh my God, I'm about to kiss Matt. But how do I feel about him? Kissing him does not mean I have to marry him. Okay …

Why didn't you tell me? demands my mother's voice.

OHMYGOD.

That in Vegas you …

I've got to get in there and pick it up before Matt hears.

… got marr…

I dive the last three metres to knock the phone off the hook.

'MUM!' I scream into the handset – the machine clicking off.

Rachel?

'Hi Mum,' I smile up at Matt who's looking a little shell-shocked.

Are you alright? he mouths. I nod, pull my track pants back up and take the kitchen stool off my chest.

I point outside. 'I'm just going to take this call outside.' Waaaaaay outside. Sitting behind Dad's car in the garage, whispering, outside.

What was that crash I heard? asks Patricia.

'Nothing,' I say. 'I knocked over a chair.'
A chair?
'Okay, then, a plant.'
A plant? Which plant? Not my orchid, I hope?
'Look it's fine, Mum. So, you got my message? About Troy? About the Vegas thing?'

Patricia is unnervingly calm. She says that she and Dad and Caitlin all understand. That she wishes that I had told her at the time. That the key now is just to get the divorce and move on. Life's too short. Who cares? All that kind of thing. And was I aware of the Bride of the Year Pageant?

'I'll talk to you about this when you get home.'
Rachel?
'Yeah, Mum?'
Whatever you do, your father and I love you. This isn't as bad as it seems. You did what you thought was the right thing at the time. Don't worry. Okay?
'Okay. Thanks, Mum.'
I walk back inside.
So, you kinda have telephone issues, huh?
'So, let's get a pizza.'

45

I look at my watch for the third time in two minutes. There are entrants just milling around, networking. They've brought family members and boyfriends with them. I just want them to hurry up and get this show on the road.

I feel a hand on my shoulder.

Hola chicka.

'Oh my God. Zoë, what are you doing here?' And then I notice that Alex and Sharon are standing behind her.

Oh you know, we thought you needed some moral support.

Sharon and Alex give me a good luck hug and Sharon whispers in my ear, *I rang Fergus to see how you were going and topped up your fundraising — think of it as an early Christmas bonus.* And then she and Alex go in search of the toilets.

Oh God.

I can't believe you didn't get out of this, Hill, says Zoë, once Alex and Sharon have disappeared.

'Don't even say "I told you so". I'm just counting on the other Corinda District entrant having raised more money than me.'

And if she hasn't?

'Well, then I'm going to bow out gracefully, saying that I think the other entrant would probably be better than me. Deserves it more. Would be a better representative …'

Oh, you're going to bullshit them.

'Pretty much.'

I don't think you've got anything to worry about.

'I hope not.'

I finally see Fergus in the corner of the room talking to Jan. He looks pretty much how I expected him to look. Like Joey Perrone with a perm.

Zoë looks around at the crowd of malnourished entrants.

Too many freaks, not enough circuses. Wanna bet that you're the only entrant who still gets her period?

'Zee! Shh.'

I practise in my head my 'it's not you, it's me' speech. Zoë argues with the waiter about whether tequila slammers can be classed as basic spirits, claiming that it's a slap in the face to a Mexican to say that tequila isn't on the list.

And then, just as Fergus takes the microphone, Alex and Sharon take their seats and the proceedings begin.

I'd like to thank you all for coming along this evening. And most of all I'd like to thank our entrants and their families for coming this evening for the announcement of which girls will be proceeding into the next round of the Miss Brisbane Awards.

We clap.

As you know, tonight we will be announcing the names of the entrants who will be representing the twelve districts of Brisbane. For those of you who don't make it through, we'd like to thank you for your efforts and we'll be presenting you with a special certificate commemorating your time with the awards.

More clapping.

Okay, we're going to start with the Corinda District. We have Rachel Hill from Kenmore who raised $501.35 cents.

Alex and Sharon and Zoë start cheering.

Oh God. Oh God. Oh God.

And then Zoë says, *Your nails are digging into my arm.*

'Sorry.'

But the winner is Zoë Budd of Taringa, who raised $3,658.84.

'WHAT?'

Alex, Sharon and I stare open-mouthed at Zoë.

Tell you later, says Zoë, not moving her lips as she smiles at the crowd. She gets up.

'Zoë!' I grab her arm.

After the RE, I took your $300 bucks and got lucky on Black Jack at the Casino.

'But I …'

Rach, my public is calling me.

Time, tide and lesbian beauty pageant entrants wait for no one. And I watch Zoë Budd stride up to the microphone.

Thanks – thank you, really, thanks, she says, trying to calm the applause.

And as she woos the crowd with her wit and charm, I realise with horror and fascination that she's never looked more at home. I have no doubt that this city is about to get its first lesbian porn-writing Miss Brisbane.

In the car on the way home, I am still in shock.

'I can't believe you did that. Why didn't you tell me?'

Consider it your birthday present.

'But you know you're going to have to raise $5000 to qualify for the final. You're going to have to do heaps of fundraising, try and get yourself in the paper, turn up to heaps of events with the other entrants …'

Oh my God – a job that involves 24-hour attention and being surrounded by beautiful women is like Zoë's dream job.

'You were born to do this, weren't you?'

She looks at me and smiles.

We arrive home and no sooner are we in the door than Matt is knocking it down again.

'Hey.'

So, what happened? Are you the new Miss Corinda?

Nah babe, that's me. Zoë swaggers out from the bar.

'Matt, Zoë, Zoë, Matt.'

Well, you are definitely a bit of a hottie.

Matt looks at me.

'She's harmless. She's an all-bark-no-bite lesbian.'

So YOU'RE the new Miss Corinda –

Every inch, in the flesh, service with a smile, baby, she says, smacking her arse.

Congratulations!

Thanks. Zoë helps herself to a serving of lasagne.

We each take a seat at the table.

'Hang on, I'll just get some serviettes,' I say.

So, what made you enter? I hear Matt ask Zoë.

Well, let's face it, if Rachel wasn't married I never …

I swing around.

Zoë's mouth falls open. She looks back at me in horror. And then I look at Matt. The shock in his eyes is clear.

Are you married?

'Matt, look, I just …'

Are. You. Married?

'Yes.'

So much for not keeping any secrets. And he gets up and walks out of the house.

I am so sorry, Zoë says, her face in her hands.

'It's alright, Zee. It was an accident. It's my fault, I should have told him. I just should have told him.'

46

Dear Matt
I'm married.
That sentence was fairly easy to type. But hasn't been so easy to say out loud. To you. To my parents. To myself.
I suppose I should really start by saying that I'm sorry that I didn't tell you. I have a lot of excuses. None of which, now, seem to be good enough to warrant withholding this information from you. You, who have become one of my closest friends.
His name is Troy. He lives in Los Angeles. After three years of dating, we got married in Las Vegas earlier this year so that I could get a Green Card and move to the US

to be with him. We didn't tell anyone. We were planning to keep it a secret and then get married "properly" down the track. I got married in shorts and a T-shirt and then came back here alone, quit my job and prepared for my big move to the USA.
Needless to say none of that happened. I am here. Troy is over there. He changed his mind. Wants a divorce. So I have been sitting here for the last month or so, nursing divorce papers, and playing that stupid piano like a woman possessed.
Who would have thought that it would lead me to you?
I really am sorry that I didn't tell you. Some days I just plain used to forget that I was married. And some days, when I did remember, I didn't want to admit it. Talk about it out loud. I think that I thought talking about it would make it more real.
A truth: Rachel Hill screwed up.
Does any of this take away the anger that you feel toward me right now? Probably not. But know this. I care about you. A lot. I don't want to lose you over this.
Forgive me. Please.
Rachel

Much later on Tuesday night I venture over to Matt's house and push this letter under his front door. When I get home the phone starts ringing. I pray that it's Matt. It's not. It's

Anne Sneddon. Shit. My heart sinks. I am about to get a fundraising lecture. Except that I don't. She doesn't mention Miss Brisbane. Or any event involving crowns and sceptres. She says she heard through my parents recently that I was doing freelance writing. She says that she's familiar with my work. She says that her company produces newsletters for different organisations and they could use a good freelancer to cover a range of stories. She wonders if I would be interested in some regular work?

'Absolutely.'

Three days pass and I hear nothing from Matt. I guess he has made his decision. Can't forgive me.

I concentrate on looking after Alex, preparing her for Saturday's concert. I take on the role of Zoë's fundraising manager and help her plan her first charity movie night. I ring Caitlin and we talk properly about where we're both at. And I post the divorce papers back to the US divorce lawyers. As clichéd and obvious as it sounds I feel a shift inside me, like the second wave is coming. A fresh start.

I decide to celebrate my last day as a twenty-seven-year-old with a piece of hummingbird cake and a pot of tea.

What type of tea do you want? Earl Grey, English Breakfast? The Coffee Club waitress has that early morning perkiness that I've always strived for.

'Oh, um, Earl Grey I think.'

She nods and starts speed-typing on the cash register. She hands me a table number.

'And I take it white. With two sugars.'

Right, well there's a sugar bowl on the table, she says, without looking up from the till.

'That's great. Because, you know, I take two sugars.'

She looks up, confused, as if I'm her first ever slightly mad, sweet-toothed customer. *Sit anywhere you like.*

I choose a table that is partly in the sun. And as I sit here, I realise that I'm happy. And it doesn't matter that I haven't quite worked out where it is I'm going yet. That I've made a few mistakes. That I only have $97.35 in the bank. That I have a drawer full of bedazzled tea-towels. Because things are going to get better for me. And right now, right this very minute, I'm surviving. Happy. Single. I have job prospects. And I pull out the pen and paper that I packed in my bag before I left the house.

Things to Achieve Before I Turn Forty
Learn basic Italian.
Visit Madrid.
Take art lessons.
Buy a huge reading chair.
Lose five kilos.
Buy my first apartment.
Write a novel.

I look at the list.

Here you go, one pot of Earl Grey tea. And you know where the sugar bowl is. The waitress laughs. This catches me by surprise. I smile back at her.

My nanna has four.

I look up at the waitress. 'Four?'

Spoonfuls of sugar! She pulls a face and laughs out loud.

This time I laugh with her. Then I look back down at the page in front of me and I rip it off the pad and screw it up into a tight little ball.

Do you want me to put it in the bin for you?

'Umm.' I hold the little ball in my hand. 'Yeah. Yeah, that would be good.' And I hand her my little scrunched up list of expectations.

No worries. She turns to go but then stops in her tracks. *Are you a writer?* I see her staring at my notebook and pen.

'Umm, yeah. I am. I'm a writer.'

Cool.

'Yeah, it is pretty cool.' And I pour myself a really sweet cup of tea.

47

My *feet hurt.*

'I know. Just try not to think about it.'

I'm thirsty. My mouth is really, really dry.

I look at Sharon and roll my eyes. 'Well, hang on and in just a second I'll buy you a Coke.'

How long is this going to take?

'Zoë! We promised Alex that we'd watch her concert. So just be quiet or I'll send you to the car.' I look through the crowd. 'I can't see Matt anywhere.'

Do you even know if he read the letter? Sharon says, offering Zoë and I some chewing gum.

I have another look through the sea of heads around me.

'No. Haven't heard a word from him. Keep your eyes

peeled for him, though. Because he'll be here. He promised Alex he'd come and watch her today.'

He'll be here. We're friends. He'll have read my letter and calmed down a bit. Maybe. What if he hasn't, though? What if THIS IS IT? Shit.

Are you going to say something to him? Zoë gate-crashes my thoughts.

'I don't know, Zee.'

But he knows it's your birthday today, right? You'd think that he'd at least say happy birthday to you.

'Yeah, well, maybe he thinks I've got a husband to do that sort of thing.'

Oh, here they come. It's starting.

And out onto the Indooroopilly Shoppingtown Centre Stage come the Birch Dance Troupe for their twenty minute 'Talk to the Animals' concert. I see Alex in the crowd and wave at her. She gives us a lopsided grasshopper grin.

Sharon blows her a kiss. Zoë and I smile and wave at her through the entire performance. She waves back at me and mouths, *Hi Rachel*.

It makes me appreciate how far I've come with Alexandria Moore. These days, most days, we laugh. We play the poking game or chase each other round the table or sing along to the radio on our way home from ballet or pretend that Alex is a lion whose den looks suspiciously like two lounge chairs and a blanket. Or she sits up on the bench while I make her a Strawberry Quik and we just shoot the breeze. And she'll ask me what rain is and what a burp is made of and declare that her Digger book is boring. Other days she'll tell me her thoughts on life, like her theory that Rose deliberately pushed Jack off the wood in *Titanic* to kill him and that it was her fault that he died. And I realise that getting close to Alex was never one of my goals and yet it's given me more satisfaction and taught me more than anything else that was on that decade-old list.

The kids take their curtsies on stage. Sharon and I clap wildly. Zoë whistles with her fingers.

The crowd begins to disperse and I still see no sign of Matt. We approach the stage to see Alex, who is already in the grip of Sharon's hug.

'Hey you, good work! You were fantastic.'

She grins and gives me a giant hug. *Did you see me wave, Rachel?*

'I certainly did! You were the prettiest girl up there!'

Look what Matt gave me, she says, pointing to two pink hairclips hidden away under her grasshopper hat.

'When did he?'

There he is! Zoë nudges my arm and points off into the distance, where Matt is making his way back through the shopping centre.

'Matt! MATTHEW! MATTHEW!'

But he continues to walk, unable to hear me because of the crowds.

'MATT! MATTHEW!'

He keeps walking, getting further and further away. I need to talk to him. I have to talk to him. Now.

Chase after him, Zoë says, pushing me in the shoulders.

'I'll never reach him,' I say, watching him disappear.

Then I look up on stage. I get an idea.

'Zee, give me a lift up will you?'

Zoë hoists me onto the stage and I scramble to my feet and grab a microphone, which has been left on the top of a piano.

Hill! What are you doing?

My heart starts to race. I take a few deep breaths. I sit down on the piano stool.

Hill! What on earth …

I turn the mike on.

I clear my throat.

And I start to hum the *Mork and Mindy* theme song over the Indooroopilly Shoppingtown PA system. I hum it loud. And sure, slightly off-key. But I hum that damn song with the gusto usually reserved for the pre-State-Of-Origin national anthem.

I can feel hundreds of eyes on me. But my eyes stay focused on Matt's back. And I watch as the song registers in Matt's brain and he stops in his tracks outside Sportsgirl. He turns around to see me on the stage humming into the mike in front of a crowd of shoppers. He starts to laugh.

By the time I put the mike back down (and a security guard has appeared), Matt is waiting for me at the front of the stage.

At first neither of us speaks.

You know, it should be more legato. I think you sang it a bit quick.

'Oh yeah?'

Yeah.

I bite my lip.

But I know someone who's an expert at theme songs who'd be willing to give you some free lessons. You know. Just to help you get up to speed.

'What's the catch?' I ask, jumping down off the stage to stand next to him.

No catch, he says. And he takes my hand in his and we begin walking back through the centre. *Assuming you can remember the theme song to* Eight is Enough.

Acknowledgments

Thanks to my parents, Rob, Sonja, Nicky, Kai, Sarah, Justin, Penny, Shaun, Katrina, Madonna, Robyn, Jude and Michael, Sally, Dan, Jo (and the Bat), Jane and Parker, Lindsay and Kylie, Scott, Raewyn, Jason, Nova and Rowena, Tina, Julie and Tanya, Maria and the Katie — my unofficial cheer-squad. Thanks also to the 2000 class of 7C at Indooroopilly State School for constantly telling me that I was amazing and that they liked my hair.

Big thanks to Allison "Rusho" Rushby for her continuous support (both on and off the treadmill) and for trying to make me stick to her "no pajamas after eleven am" rule. And to David for not giving me any advice whatsoever.

To KOB for sitting where you did in that youth hostel in Salzburg. To Anne Sneddon who let a little girl with bad hair dream big! And to Alleshia for showing me life through the eyes of a six year old.

Heartfelt thanks to Jessica Adams, Clare Forster and Carol Davidson who gave lots of encouragement. And to Rebekah Scott and everyone at UQP for hard work behind the scenes – in particular I consider myself very lucky to have had Madonna Duffy as my publisher.

But the biggest thanks must go to my good friend and mentor Nick Earls for doing the occasional Scottish accent (á la *Finding Forrester*) during my low moments but more importantly for putting up with the part A and B moments, the long phone calls, the high drama and for always believing that I could do it. Thank you for sharing your enormous talent and for having the vision (and patience) to pass on the torch and encourage other writers who are just starting out.

This book is dedicated to the memory of my Nanna, Annie Jeffery, who with a mischievous gleam in her eye, smoked, drank, watched *Days of Our Lives* and fed the dog at the table. Thank you for inspiring me.

And to Rosie, with love.

Other fiction by

UQP

I KNIT WATER
Craig Bolland

Runner-up 2001 Queensland Premier's Literary Awards

Meet Mark Heron ... twenty-something, burned out and recently washed up at the West End house they call Heartbreak Lodge.

Meet his new neighbours ... Steve, who won a local art prize and hasn't been able to finish a painting since; Agnes, who looks like Malibu Barbie but dresses like a 40s schoolmarm; Dave, optimist, idealist, connoisseur of 'Star Wars' memorabilia and hard core porn; Sarah, compassionate mystic with a checkered past; Speedy, a tri-sexual Vietnam vet; Trix, rave chick diva and professional nutcracker; Errol, ex-Olympic fencer, sliding into old age and dementia.

Mark's life becomes interwoven with his fellow tenants, their stories overlaying to form pieces of a whole. As events unfold that threaten to turn their world upside down, Mark finds he must either go under ... or learn to knit water.

This novel is intelligent, insightful and above all movingly honest.
Judges' Report — Best Emerging Queensland Author
2001 Queensland Premier's Literary Awards

ISBN 0 7022 3319 6

HER SISTER'S EYE
Vivienne Cleven

'... Always remember where you're from ...'

To the Aboriginal families of Mundra, this saying brings either comfort or pain. To Nana Vida it is what binds the generations. To the unwilling savant Archie Corella it portends a fate too cruel to name. For Sophie Salte, whose woman's body and child's mind make her easy prey, nothing matters while her sister Murilla is there to watch over her.

For Murilla, fierce protector and unlikely friend to Caroline Drysdale, wife of the town patriarch, what matters is survival. In a town with a history of vigilante raids, missing persons and unsolved murders, survival can be all that matters.

These stories — of the camp, the boy and his snake, the shooting — told and passed on, offer a release from the horrors of our past. As Nana Vida says,

'That's the story. I let it go now.'

Vivienne Cleven's first book *Bitin' Back* won the 2000 David Unaipon Award, was shortlisted in the 2001 South Australian Premier's Literary Awards, and was shortlisted for the 2002 *Courier-Mail* Book of the Year Award.

This is a brilliant literary novel. Through Cleven's strongly developed characters, her use of magical elements and the novel's disquieting sense of place, she offers a powerful and sensitive look at Australia's treatment of not only indigenous people but also of women.

Chris Stamenitis, *Australian Bookseller and Publisher*

ISBN 0 7022 3283 1

UQP

THE HARD WORD
John Clanchy

Vera, Miriam, Laura — one family, three generations — with Miriam at the centre, balancing the needs of her mother and daughter with those of her marriage and career.

Vera is slipping into the darkness of Alzheimer's disease, while Laura is embroiled in teenage conflicts of identity and sexuality.

In her professional life, Miriam is able to help others unlock the past through the simple power of words. So, what prevents her from doing it for those closest to her? And for herself ...?

The answer to this painful dilemma emerges not so much from within Miriam herself, but from the hard, raw experience of the migrant and refugee women she teaches. Their stories resonate with her own, and she finds herself sustained in her own crisis by their strength and laughter.

In this sensitive exploration of memory, love and family, John Clanchy's writing reaches new levels of insight, while retaining distinctive humour.

Clanchy explores the big questions like love, death, betrayal and loss with a rare toughness and an even rarer insight ... He is a highly accomplished writer.

Mark Henshaw, *Canberra Times*

This is a novel about family life ... The narrative shape of the novel follows two processes in two lives, namely Laura's adolescent blossoming and Grandma Vera's decline: the gentle despair and savage comedy of Vera's condition recall Geoffrey Atherden's great scripts for Mother and Son.

Kerryn Goldsworthy, *Weekend Australian*

ISBN 0 7022 3332 3

UQP

IN ONE SKIN
Kristina Olsson

Evelyn and Elena are sisters, 'fiercely close'. Growing up without a mother, they have nourished each other, creating their own versions of reality.

Now Evelyn is missing, and the certainties of Elena's adult life are shattered. Daily routine no longer soothes her; the cocoon of safety she has woven around her husband and two sons no longer seems enough.

In Evelyn's diary, she can find no trace of the sister she knew. Anger and blame, the pull of memory and blood fill its terrifying pages. Only by facing the buried secrets of her own life can Elena reach a hard-won understanding of her sister — and herself.

The profound consequences of abandonment and the promise of renewal are all deftly explored here in language that pierces the heart. *In One Skin* is an elegant and evocative novel that reveals the hooks and ties of family life.

My favourite book this year was In One Skin ... *I like it because I love stories about relationships and love and kids and the general mess of people's lives. The language is beautiful. It's a 'read-at-one-sitting' job.*

Marg O'Donnell, Director-General, Arts Queensland

ISBN 0 7022 3271 8

UQP

GODDESS AND THE GALAXY BOY
Ingrid Woodrow

Shortlisted for the *Australian*/Vogel award 2001

Ingrid Woodrow's wild journey of grinding collision and hilarious near-misses propels us along a Pacific Highway of her imagination.

When Galaxy Boy and his one-armed friend Houdini speed headlong into Goddess's life, she confronts a new world of possibilities and dangerously eccentric characters.

She takes her story, fits it with fourteen-by-eight-inch mags, a flare kit and a Chevy 350 V8, puts the pedal to the metal and here it comes.

Nick Earls, author of *Zigzag Street* and *Bachelor Kisses*

Woodrow is a gifted character writer. Indeed, at times she seems to portray the inner lives of her feckless drifters with the sort of effortless skill that recalls a Raymond Carver ... In the character of Goddess, Woodrow has created an immensely likeable young woman with real plausibility to her, the sort of character readers will turn pages for — a worthy heroine, in short.

Ben Eltham, *Courier-Mail*

This is an hilarious and hair-raising road novel, with appealing characters and an ingenious structure.

Gillian Dooley, *Australian Book Review*

ISBN 0 7022 3211 4

UQP

MACHINES FOR FEELING
Mireille Juchau

Shortlisted 2000 *Australian*/Vogel Award

Rien meets Mark at St Mary's Home for Children. They experience passion, loss and hope as they begin a tenuous but tender relationship and a new life beyond the Home. While Mark dreams of machines to repair their fractured world, Rien writes stories of falling to help her recover the missing events of her past. Their friend, Dog Boy, escapes from St Mary's to embark on a ragged journey that will dramatically alter each of their lives.

Mireille Juchau writes with a strong spare poetic style. In creating three unusual characters with distinctly inventive inner lives, she raises questions about the nature of being and individuality and highlights the enduring power of the imagination in a world with little time for difference, or patience for sensitivity.

The prose sings with a luminiscent clarity and evocativeness.

Judges' Report — *Australian*/Vogel Award

Often unexpectedly funny, with a clean bare style and constant points of pleasure.

Brenda Walker

ISBN 0 7022 3218 1

UQP